MW01222748

"Allen Unrau's ⟨
what was The ⟨
(when the pape
2005 to 2008. The section—for which I was editor at
the time—provided a balance to the more hard-hitting
news that filled the front pages, with features and
general-interest stories about the people, places and
events that make the community tick. Allen's column
was the perfect fit, with his innate ability to capture
heartwarming, heartbreaking and humorous snippets
of life in a relatable and comforting way. Don't be
surprised if, after reading some of his stories, you feel
inclined to call your mom or hug your grandpa. Such is
the magic of Allen's writing.
   – Vikki Hopes, Abbotsford News reporter since 1991

"Your articles in the paper are like a breath of fresh air
amidst all the disturbing news. I always clip the
articles and take them to my disabled daughter. I read
them to her, and we enjoy them together." – A.W.

"We always enjoy your articles, but this one was
particularly effective. I'm sure every seasoned reader
can recall a family that has been affected by a very
similar situation." – M.O.

"Thank you for painting such a sensitive picture of
what loneliness looks like for many people." –S.C.

"Thank you for running Allen Unrau's column. I think I
speak for a lot of people when I say that it helps
restore people's faith in the ability of strangers to
empathize with each other. In an age when people are
increasingly alienated from people around them, the
characters in Allen's column remind us that the
strangers around us are not so different from us. The

situations his characters find themselves in remind us that strangers around us experience the same kind of wonder and confusion we do. In many ways, his stories are a surrogate for the type of close-knit communities that a lot of us miss." – B.W.

"I thoroughly enjoy the stories written by Allen Unrau. I search the paper for his column and pass it on. I have discovered that anyone I have mentioned these articles to has also read and enjoyed them. These articles educate and entertain us." – L.M.

"Thank you for choosing Allen Unrau to write those wonderful, insightful stories. His articles are a tremendous asset to your paper, often close to being tear-jerkers." – A.D.

"Allen Unrau has a unique understanding of human nature and especially the problems and thought processes of seniors. His column helps us to understand both ourselves and our fellow seniors just a little better." – J.W.

"To be able to introduce characters, tell a story, and bring it to a satisfactory conclusion in 600 words is a remarkable ability. To be able at the same time to expand understanding, tickle the funny bone, encourage the heart, turn on smiles and bring the reader to tears is an astonishing feat. Yet this is what Allen Unrau achieves in these highly readable slices of life." – James R. Coggins, writer and editor

Five-Minute Slices of Life

The Collected Stories of
Allen Unrau

Mill Lake Books

Enjoy.

Al Unrau

Published by Mill Lake Books
Chilliwack, BC
Canada
jamescoggins.wordpress.com/mill-lake-books

Cover design by Dean Tjepkema

Printed by Lightning Source, distributed by Ingram

ISBN: 978-1-998787-03-6

Table of Contents

Put him in soft soil

Peter's right thumb twitches uncontrollably as his daughter Erika takes his hand. It used to be calloused and rough like coarse sandpaper. Now it's weak, soft and limp.

"I'm right here, Father. I won't leave you. Are you thirsty?"

Peter Kozma is dying after a life of seeming insignificance. He immigrated here after the war and worked at the plywood plant for forty-three years.

He's over ninety and hasn't spoken for weeks.

"Father, is there anything you want to say to me?"

No response.

At 3:00 a.m., Peter becomes restless and agitated. His eyes flutter open for short periods of time as he kicks at the sheets and squeezes the bedrail.

"Father, is there anything I can do for you?"

Struggling to breathe, he finally opens his mouth to speak. Anticipating his last words, she leans over him as he mumbles weakly in Hungarian, "Let me lie in the soil of my village."

Then, Peter's body relaxes, and his eyes close permanently.

"Did you hear him speak to me?" she asks the nurse making her rounds.

"Yes, but I don't understand the language."

"He asked to be buried in Hungary. Is that even possible?"

The palliative care nurse replies mechanically, "Airlines transporting corpses out of the country require that the body be embalmed and shipped in a hermetically sealed container. You'll need a death certificate, an embalming report, his passport, a burial permit and a letter from his doctor stating that he did not die from a communicable disease. It's very expensive."

Now, Erika wrestles with his last request. Did he really mean it? He had never even been back to Hungary. Is this what he's wanted all along? Or was it just the heavy medication talking?

She had planned a small funeral and reserved a plot next to his brother in the local cemetery. The money he's left her will cover expenses and leave only a small nest egg.

Erika asks her family lawyer for advice. His response: "Dying people sometimes make impossible requests. You can't always take them seriously."

It's what Erika was hoping he would say. She can't take any more time off work. Certainly, her father would understand.

But Erika can't find peace. The words "the soil of my village" constantly run through her mind. Finally, out of frustration, she decides to honor his last request, secretly hoping things won't work out and she can still bury him here.

One week later, after a tedious overseas flight, unusual requests for paperwork and unexpected expenses, she boards a train leaving Budapest. Village officials have been notified that she's bringing his body back.

The cemetery is a small, tree-enclosed site on the side of a knoll next to a potato field. Many of the gravestones are faded and worn, and some have sunk deeply into the ground.

An aging caretaker shuffles out of the village. He's followed by a strong, teenaged boy carrying a shovel. In Hungarian he asks Erika, "Where do you want him?"

She breaks down, thinking she's made a terrible mistake bringing him here. "Put him in soft soil, under a tree. He loved trees."

As the grave is dug, a crowd begins to form at the tiny cemetery. Soon, hundreds surround the gravesite. Children place flowers on his coffin, and families offer Erika their homes for lodging. Bowing in respect, a weathered older man offers Erika a crystal jar of walnuts in golden acacia honey.

A local priest speaks to the crowd. "We are gathered to honor the life of Peter Kozma, who risked his life to save many of our families during the war. And then he was gone. He is worthy of our extreme gratitude."

Erika, kneeling in the soft soil, looks up in wonder at the crowd around her. The older men are removing their woolen caps and saluting her father's coffin. The new, black shovel, still dusted with soil, is wrapped in a white, knitted shawl and presented to Erika.

Investment of a lifetime

Art and Lillian Turner sit quietly in the waiting room of the law office of Marsolais and Company. They have come to sign documents to transfer their home.

Dark glasses hide Lillian's swollen eyes. Art is slumped in a chair beside her, his spirit broken. They've lost everything after forty-seven years of marriage. Their house, their investments and their savings are all gone.

Rose, a legal assistant, shows them to the boardroom. She deposits a series of files on the table and leaves quietly. They are nice people, and she's sensitive to their sadness.

Art and Lillian are victims of a Ponzi scheme. They invested heavily in "guaranteed" mortgages with Chartex Investment Corp., which promised three times the interest the bank was paying. Lillian's cousin bought in. Soon, he was driving a brand new motorhome. Must be OK, they figured.

Their lawyer, James Marshall, enters the room. "I wish I could offer hope that you will recover some of your investment. Chartex has collapsed. Your money is gone."

Art speaks slowly. "How could we have been so foolish? I only wanted to make sure we had enough money for our retirement."

The Turners leave the law office in tears, their financial security wiped out.

Their children help them move to a rental house at 74691 Maple Crescent. Old friends of the family have offered them a reasonable monthly rate for a solid, well-maintained rancher a few blocks from their old home.

The moving van arrives with what's left of their possessions. "Mom, we'll make this place feel like home," says daughter Susan.

Lillian puts on a brave face, but she's heartbroken. This is not her home. It never will be.

Six months later, the Turners receive another call from Rose at the law office. "We have some legal papers for you to sign. Mr. Marshall would like to see you at eleven o'clock on Tuesday."

More legal documents to drain their lives even further. Art and Lillian are getting used to it. This appointment doesn't seem unusual.

As their lawyer enters the room, Lillian recognizes the scent of his Gucci cologne. It used to mean success. Now it reminds her of disaster. Lawyers' offices are sweet and sour.

"Good morning, folks. I've prepared some land title transfer documents. The property is being transferred into both your names."

Art is puzzled. "What are you talking about? We haven't acquired any property." He's upset they've been dragged in to sign documents that were obviously prepared for someone else.

"Mr. and Mrs. Turner, you've been gifted with a home. The current owners of 74691 Maple Crescent signed the transfer documents this morning."

Art Turner examines the transfer documents carefully. "None of this makes any sense. We are only renting this place. I must speak to our landlords. Could you get them on the phone?"

Their lawyer gets up and opens the door. "Better yet, I'll bring them in. They've asked to speak with you."

Darin and Julie Davis are in their mid-forties and operate a highly successful fruit-processing plant. Hillcrest Farms' jams and jellies are sold around the world.

Julie starts; "We're here today to finish some old family business. Mr. Turner, when I was just a kid, you loaned my father $2,600 to buy his first orchard. The bank wouldn't give him the money. You gave it to him in cash. He paid it back as agreed, but he always told us we wouldn't have the financial success we've enjoyed as a family if it wasn't for your kindness."

Julie rests her hand on Lillian's shoulder. "It's payback time. The home on Maple Crescent is now yours, no strings attached. You earned it thirty-five years ago."

It's a bad day when you lose a hundred dollars

Erin Gregory is paying her rent at the property manager's office.

She pulls cash from the side pocket of her pink nylon diaper bag. The cashier counts the bills. "You're a hundred dollars short, Miss Gregory." She looks through the records. "You have been chronically late. This time, you can expect an eviction notice."

Erin grabs the money and counts it herself. It's true. There's a hundred missing. She's horrified.

"It was all there when I got on the bus this morning. I counted it twice before I left."

Desperately, she digs through her bag. The money is gone.

Office staff give her looks of mistrust. Typical renter's story. They've heard it all before.

Erin's baby starts to cry.

She leaves the money on the counter, gathers up little Ariana and starts for the door. "I've got to find it. I'll be back as soon as I do."

She runs back to the bus stop, searching the sidewalks along the way and inspecting paper trash of all sorts. The corner of a potato chip bag catches her eye, giving temporary hope. It's the right color only. The bus stop is crowded now. No chance there.

The walk back to the property manager's office is agony, her eyes penetrating the shrubbery and scanning the fence lines.

"Did you lose something?" An older gentleman approaches her from the parking lot. He looks to be late sixties, wearing a golf shirt and slacks.

"I lost a hundred dollars," Erin replies sharply, thinking he probably won't believe her anyway.

"Was it five twenties?"

"No, it was a hundred-dollar bill. I earned it babysitting for my neighbor. Now it's gone, and I can't pay my rent. The office lady says I'll be evicted."

Her baby hasn't stopped crying. Little ones feel their mothers' tension. Erin can't hold it any longer and bursts into tears. "All the doors are closing for me. I just turned twenty-five. I'm trying to be a good mother. I'm going to Conroy College part time. In three months, I'll have my health care food service certificate. My budget's been stretched to the last dollar since I had the baby. I didn't plan this. I feel so alone. If it wasn't for little Ariana, I don't know what I might do."

"I'm sorry to hear about your situation. My name is Frank Hayes. Let me tell you what happened to me this morning."

He leads her to a bench at the side of the building. "I came here to re-insure my motorhome. Cross Country Insurance is on the second floor. I spotted a hundred-dollar bill on the sidewalk. 'My lucky day', I thought. 'I'm golfing at ten. This will pay my green fees and buy lunch for all my buddies.'"

She grabs his arm. "You found my hundred? Why didn't you just leave? Most people would."

"Why isn't important right now," Frank replies. "Let's get your rent paid. I'll come in with you and confirm you had all the money when you left home."

Another month goes by. Same situation. Erin is barely scraping by. Sixty days from now, she'll have her certificate and a full-time job.

On the last day of the month, Erin packs her baby into the rental office and pulls a sealed *Ziplock* out of her diaper bag. Confidently, she counts out the cash in front of the reception clerk.

The clerk rolls back her chair and checks Erin's file. She leafs through some hand-written notes, and then closes it quickly.

"Your rent's already been paid, Miss Gregory. Actually, you're paid up for three full months."

"Who paid it?" questions Erin.

"An older fellow in a blue Nike golf shirt. Said he knew you."

Better get a good pre-nup

Christine Albinati is leafing through a stack of brides' magazines. At forty-six, this will be her second marriage.

She's asked her mother and sisters to help with the wedding plans. They are fretting, disappointed that she's getting married so soon after Larry's death and suspicious of her new husband-to-be.

"Does he know you got a big life insurance settlement?" asks her sister.

"I've told him that I'm financially secure. He didn't ask many questions."

Her mother speaks up. "He's not stupid. He's figured out you've got money. I think he's a gold-digger."

Her younger sister jumps in. "I can't believe this guy's never been married. Forty-eight? C'mon. He's a phony."

Her older sister paces the room. "You'd better get a good pre-nup signed."

Christine replies confidently, "I've already signed one. His lawyer prepared it. Burke said there were some things that needed to be addressed because of his family business and he wanted me to be fully protected if something should happen to him."

Outbursts from all of them: "You are blindly in love." "You'll get hurt." "He'll say whatever it takes to get at your money." "This guy's a predator."

Christine is undisturbed. "He loves me. I can tell. I've always trusted my intuition."

Her family leaves without the usual hugs. If she marries this man, she's on her own.

Where did this relationship start?

Three months ago, Christine arrived at the airport early for a flight to Toronto to see her daughter in university. From her spot in the check-in line, she heard a woman weeping at the far end of the terminal: a young Inuit woman with a tiny baby.

As she approached the woman, Christine caught a musky whiff of Arctic life. Christine tried to calm her, but the distressed mother obviously didn't speak English. She seemed totally lost in this world of glass, gift shops and red plastic seats.

A middle-aged man approached: gray-blond hair, kindly blue eyes, brown leather jacket and jeans.

"I'm Burke. She's speaking Inuktitut. I spent many summers in the Arctic as a boy. Maybe I can help."

He knelt beside the sobbing mother, took her hand and spoke slowly. Her face brightened, and she responded. He stood up. "She brought her baby down for surgery. Someone from the hospital was to meet them at the gate but didn't show up."

Burke made a phone call, and Christine and Burke stayed with her until an apologetic nurse arrived. Poor communication about flight times from Rankin Inlet.

Burke picked up his briefcase, then slowly turned back to Christine. "There's still an hour until my flight. Would you join me at Starbucks?"

*****

The wedding is a private ceremony with only immediate family attending. The finest French cuisine and exotic orchids.

Burke's father proposes a toast. "Burke, your mother and I were beginning to wonder if this would ever happen. You told me years ago you would never marry until you were certain. Christine, you were worth waiting for!"

A news report the following Monday explains: *Thomas Burke Billings, 48, has wed 46-year-old Christine Albinati in a private ceremony at the Billings family estate. Burke is the only heir to the Billings Oil and Gas fortune. The Billings family amassed their wealth through exploration in the Canadian Arctic. Christine Albinati is a widow who has been working for a local dentist. Burke describes her as "the first woman who ever accepted me for who I was, without knowing I was a Billings.*

The forty-eight-hour fight

With his arms pinned by his sides, he is powerless to stop the insects crawling around the corners of his eyes. He squints and twitches. Still, they move across his face.

After a fight with his wife, Paul Kidd took off his wedding ring, got on his Harley-Davidson and rode it far too fast on his favorite stretch of mountain road.

This is what he does lately when he's angry with Stacey. Riding the banked curves and rolling hills of Highway 14A at twice the posted speeds gets things out of his system.

Now he's trapped face down under his Harley after clipping the corner of a steel bridge and cartwheeling down the rocky shoulder. The bottom of the ditch is cool, with thick, moist sedge grass cushioning his body from the full weight of the motorcycle. He's badly injured, and breathing is difficult.

It's 1:00 a.m.

Paul thinks, "I can't die during a forty-eight-hour fight. I always thought I would die of cancer or something where I would have some time to tell her how I felt."

The "forty-eight-hour fight" was named by their son Aaron, who is away at college.

Six months ago, they had a doozer. "You know we're in debt. There's still a-year-and-a-half left on your truck loan, and you go out and buy a new Harley?

You must be going through some whacko, male, mid-life crisis. Go see your doctor after you take that thing back to the dealer."

The "forty-eight-hour fight" is always the same. Both of them say hurtful things and bring up the past. Not so secretly, he takes off his ring, slides it into his pocket, slams the door and leaves. She's ice-cold and talks to her friends for hours on the phone as if nothing's wrong. They crowd the edges of their king-size bed and stare at opposite walls. There's never any conversation during the first twenty-four hours. That's the rule.

Near the end of the second twenty-four hours, it's fair to start making small talk.

The last time, near the forty-six-hour mark, Paul said, "I think I should take your car in to get the tires rotated. Do you want to trade vehicles?"

"Sure. My keys are on the dresser."

And then, after forty-eight hours, the fight's over, like nothing ever happened.

Now, close to losing consciousness, Paul thinks about his chances. "She probably won't start looking for me till tomorrow."

He hears a truck pull into the rest stop back at the bridge.

He cries out into the wet grass, "I'm in the ditch down here." The diesel just keeps idling.

He sees Stacey in his mind. She's holding a wrapped gift and wearing that black dress he bought her for their second anniversary. He unwraps the red foil to discover a package of Pampers. She smiles. "I think it's a boy. Should we name him Aaron?"

Paul loses consciousness.

When he wakes up in the hospital, she's there, stroking his forehead. "I woke up. It was 3:00 a.m. You weren't home. You're always home by midnight, even when you're mad. I knew something must be terribly wrong. I told the cops about that curvy road you ride."

Stacey holds out one of his tight, black leather riding gloves. "When the medics lifted the bike off, your gloved hand was in your pocket with your ring jammed over the first knuckle of your little finger."

Paul slowly lifts his naked ring finger towards her. "I didn't expect to make it. It took all the strength I had left. I wanted you to know."

Collecting money from a dead man

"We are very sorry to hear about your uncle's passing." A blonde-haired woman in a striking turquoise suit presses a card into the hand of Sybil Clark, Nigel Clark's niece.

"Thank-you," she replies. "We've been overwhelmed by the number of tributes and condolences for Uncle Nigel. We had no idea how many lives he'd touched."

Nigel was the kind of oddball uncle that family members liked but never really knew. He drove a delivery truck for Reed's Commercial Dry Cleaning all his life, made average wages but never managed to save anything. All he left behind was a badly furnished bachelor apartment and a faded brown van with one powder blue side door. Family members had to chip in to pay the funeral expenses.

As the unexpectedly large number of funeral guests make their way slowly through the oak chapel doors onto the pale green carpeting of the reception room, the blonde woman touches Sybil's arm. "Just one more thing, if you don't mind." She lowers her voice. "Your uncle owed our father money. A copy of the debt record is in the card. We'd like it cleared up as soon as possible."

Sybil gasps and steps to the side of the doorway. "You're at my uncle's funeral to collect a debt? I didn't know Uncle Nigel owed anybody anything. As a matter of fact, from what we've been hearing in the last couple of days, he gave other people money. He evidently sponsored orphans in Haiti..."

The blonde woman raises her hands in defense. "All that may be true, but that doesn't change the facts." She pulls a piece of yellow, lined notepaper from her purse. "Is this your uncle's handwriting?"

Sybil scans the notepaper. "Yes, it looks like his scrawl."

The note is dated nine months earlier and signed by both Nigel and the lender. It reads: "$1500 borrowed from Gordon Reed. Will pay back as soon as possible."

Nigel's niece questions the woman. "Your father is Gordon Reed, my uncle's former employer at Reed's Dry Cleaning? Why would my uncle borrow money from his boss and not pay him back?"

"Drinking problem? Gambling problem? I don't know, and I don't care. All I know is that your uncle owes us the money."

"Does your father know you're collecting debts at his employee's funeral?"

The woman replies, "My father passed away two months ago. I'm the executrix, just doing my family duty."

"Well, do your duty on another day. Now, please leave. We're here to grieve and honor Uncle Nigel, not to shame him."

The blonde woman rises to her full height. "This is a straightforward matter. Our father was a successful businessman who was an asset to his community. It appears that your uncle was a deadbeat who didn't pay his bills. When can our family expect payment?"

"I-I don't know…"

Nigel's niece breaks down. Other funeral guests assume she's grieving the loss of her uncle with family friends.

The elegant blonde woman stalks away.

As Nigel's niece rummages through her purse for another Kleenex, a tiny lady wearing a large-brimmed black hat approaches her. "You are Mr. Nigel's family?"

"Yes," she sniffles. "I'm his niece. How did you know him?"

"My name Pinky Fontaine. Mr. Nigel help lot people, help me. I used work in dry cleaning plant. Nine month ago, my husband go back his country, leave no money rent. Me and sons no home two month. Mr. Nigel save us."

She presses a brown envelope into Sybil's hand. "Here is dollars owe him. He said not worry pay back even though he borrow money help me. But I have more good job now. Please make nice grave on him. He is man-angel."

Seventy-five twenty-dollar bills are in the envelope.

Her father's a freak

Cindy McNear steps off the curb, searching for the familiar Crosstown Number 7. Squinting into the sun, she double-steps into the street, frantic for the bus to appear.

A hooker, slouched against the bus shelter, screams, "Back up, you stupid...!"

It's too late.

The bumper of the truck clips her thigh, flipping her high into the air. Cindy's head hits the pavement, hard.

Liquor store patrons pour into the street, surrounding her twisted, motionless body.

A black man shelters her face with a sports magazine.

Someone applies a towel to blood oozing through bleach-blonde hair.

"Don't move her!" shouts a taxi driver from the edge of the crowd. His battered yellow cab is parked sideways, blocking traffic in the lane where she lies.

Within minutes, sirens are heard, and the medics arrive.

None of it matters. Cindy is dead.

So end thirty-eight troubled years.

Baby Cindy was a gift. Owen and Shirley McNear had given up hope. Their first pregnancy had ended in a miscarriage at twelve weeks. Their second had ended with a baby boy, stillborn.

"You would be wise to avoid pregnancy." Dr. Schreiber had hesitated, knowing how badly they wanted a child. "In my opinion, it's too risky. I see numerous complications."

Shirley and Owen were fearful facing their third pregnancy. Dr. Schreiber was nervous. The birth was difficult.

Cindy was a troublesome child—defiant and combative as a six-year-old, swearing, smoking and shoplifting as a pre-teen. Suspended from Westview High School for selling dope. Sent to a center for troubled teens.

Back home from treatment, it seemed she might have changed.

There was a young man in her life.

"Good evening, Mr. McNear. I'm here to pick up Cindy. We're going to a basketball game. I'll have her home by midnight."

Norman was a nice young man from a good family. Soon they were engaged.

Within a month, she sold the diamond. "He's boring, Mom."

A postcard from Michigan told them she was on the road with a rock band drummer named Quincey.

Pregnant, she attempted an abortion and failed. Mom and Dad begged for a chance to raise the child, but Cindy insisted on adoption. "I can't look at that baby. Her father's a freak."

She scribbled a letter to the adoptive parents: "Don't ever try to contact me or my daughter. We don't exist in your world."

In spite of this, Owen and Shirley tried to locate the baby, but all information was blocked because of "birth mother instability."

Cindy was always broke. "I only need the cash for a few days. I've got my application in at three places. Please, Dad."

Mom and Dad helped when they could. Their daughter drained them. She was never home for Christmas. Her life was a circus of drugs, eating disorders and problem relationships.

At thirty-eight, she is dead on the street in front of the liquor store.

Soon, Owen will retire from his job as a machinist. Their dreams of family have vanished.

The phone rings one Saturday morning. "Mrs. McNear, I'm your granddaughter, Jennifer. Please don't hang up. I know I'm not supposed to call you, and I know you don't care that I exist. My adoptive mother showed me the letter when I turned eighteen. I just need to know where my mother is. That's all I ask. My husband James tracked you down. Please help me. We have a baby son named Noah. What am I going to tell him about his grandmother when he's older?"

One week later, the aroma of fresh-baked apple pie fills a white, two-story house on Walnut Avenue.

Owen has been standing at the curb next to the shiny metal mailbox for more than twenty minutes, ready to flag them into the drive. Shirley is on the red brick porch wiping her hands nervously on her cotton apron.

As the car door opens, Shirley runs down the steps with her arms wide open. She rushes to the passenger side. "Jennifer, we've prayed for you every day for twenty years. We didn't know what your name was, so Grandpa Owen and I just settled on a name we both liked, a name we would have picked for you. It was *Jenny.* We both prayed for little Jenny every night before we went to sleep."

Fruit and red feathers

"Mom, I picked up a few things for your trip."

Lauren lays two shopping bags on the bed.

"You bought me clothes? You know I've always picked out my own clothes, sweetheart. People have always said I'm attractive and stylish."

"I know. You've always had good fashion sense, Mother, but the years have caught up with you."

Gail can't believe what she's hearing. At sixty-four, she's still a year away from retirement age. Last month, she ended her working life with a good pension.

For the past ten years, since Frank died, she's managed everything on her own. She thought she'd been adapting to the changes in her life quite well. Now, while preparing for a guided tour of California's historical sites, she's faced with one of the harsh realities of aging—taking advice about what to wear.

Lauren continues. "You don't need to keep following the trends anymore. Everything I've read says women your age need to look more dignified. Wearing classic styles is the first step."

"Women my age? You think I look old now?" Gail steps into her walk-in closet and runs her hand across the hangers. "What's wrong with my clothes?"

"There's nothing wrong with them, Mom. You just need to start dressing your age. You're not thirty anymore. Now, you should be dressing to look elegant."

"Elegant? You want me to look elegant? I always thought 'elegant' was used to describe antique furniture. Do you want me to start wearing brown tweed with big ruby brooches and beady-eyed furry animals wrapped around my neck? Is that what you want?"

Gail closes her closet door. "Maybe a big hat with fruit and red feathers would help me look my age. Would that make you happy?"

"No, Mom. What I mean is clothes like this." Lauren holds up the outfit she's brought for her mother. Classic navy blue suit with an ivory blouse and an expensive pair of pearl earrings.

"You'll look very attractive in this, Mom. Please, just try it on. By the way, I really like the way you're doing your hair lately."

Gail stands her ground. "Don't change the subject. I'm not going to a funeral, Lauren. Certainly not my own, I hope. I'll dress the way I feel is right for me. I'm sorry for your trouble."

Lauren is her only child. Disagreements are unusual between them, but this issue has strained their relationship. Three calls a day were normal. Now, the phone doesn't ring before Gail leaves on the trip. Lauren doesn't say goodbye.

The California tour for young-at-heart seniors is Gail's first "retirement" experience. She's delighted with the new acquaintances she makes. A gentleman named Howard insists on carrying her bags. The third night of the tour, they have coffee together on the hotel patio overlooking the harbor.

The next morning, as Gail boards the coach, she stumbles and falls. Her vision is blurred, and she has difficulty speaking. An ambulance rushes her to a local hospital. She's admitted with paralysis on her left side.

Even with Gail in the hospital, the coach tour must continue. Howard volunteers to stay with her until her daughter Lauren arrives on the first available flight.

The next day, Lauren rushes into the hospital room. Her mother recognizes her but isn't able to speak.

Tears flow.

"Mom, I'm so sorry I didn't call you."

Howard introduces himself and describes Gail's tragic fall down the bus steps.

"We were having a wonderful time getting to know each other." His voice catches as he continues. "For our group dinner party the night before last, she was wearing a blue outfit with pearl earrings. She looked so dignified and refined. Your mother is a very elegant woman."

Kermit the memory bug

"Mrs. Daley, I'm Neil, from the salvage yard. Your VW Bug is on my truck. Where should I drop it?"

"Just lift it over the back fence. I'm sure it's still too wide to go through the gate."

Jolene Daley walks into the backyard of her townhome to direct the driver. She's late forties with styled ash-blonde hair, a navy business suit and black leather pumps.

The crane lifts a cube of crushed green metal high in the air, then lowers it onto the patio next to her barbecue.

As the driver unhooks the chains, he remarks, "Not much left of this one. Your husband need it for parts?"

"I don't have a husband now."

"You work on old cars? You don't seem the type."

"This is Kermit, my very first car. A miracle happened as I was driving to the office last week. I was in the left lane, and there he was, right beside me on a flat-deck truck underneath a bunch of other squashed cars. It gave me shivers to realize that it was really him. The color of lime-green sherbet with my memories still stuck to his back bumper. I followed him to the yard. The clerk said they didn't sell wrecks to the public, but I persisted."

She bends down and points to the chrome back bumper, the only part still intact. Three faded decals. A yellow daisy coming out of the "F" in San Francisco,

33

a purple peace sign and a red "Kelsey College" parking permit.

"It was fate that I got him back."

"This isn't a VW Bug anymore, Mrs. Daley. It's just scrap. Why would you want it in your backyard?"

"Kermit was a loyal friend. I loved his cute, round eyes, his 'bneep bneep' horn and the way his beige vinyl seats smelled on hot days."

"It sounds like you were really happy back then."

"Those were the best years of my life. All I've got now is my job."

At that moment, a white-haired man with a black vinyl binder steps through her back gate. James Richter, strata president. A group of concerned neighbors press in behind him. "I'm here to enforce strata rule number 3A concerning 'undriveable' vehicles," he says. "You are hereby given notice to remove this unsightly piece of junk."

Jolene turns to the white-haired man. "Kermit is family to me."

"I always thought you to be an intelligent woman," replies the president. "Remove it immediately."

The neighbors disperse quickly, shaking their heads. A red-haired woman comments, "Lady sure is strange since her husband left."

"Mrs. Daley," the truck driver says, "can I talk to you in private?"

They step into her sunroom, and she closes the sliding door.

"Mrs. Daley, we own the salvage yard. I had a red TransAm when I was eighteen. It was everything to me. My little brother drove it without asking and wrapped it around a pole. He died. My family wanted to dispose of the wreck right away. I said no, it's part of my life. But, when I got to work a week after the funeral, it had disappeared into the shredder."

Jolene looks up. "So, you know how I feel right now?"

"Sort of. But I also know you can be happy again. Memories are only a small part of who you really are."

With Jolene sobbing, Neil wraps the chains around the crushed green cube and hoists it back onto the truck deck.

Two weeks later, a rectangular package arrives at Jolene's door from Consolidated Salvage. It's Kermit's rear bumper, decals and all, turned into a wall shelf with easy-to-install mounting brackets.

The card reads:

Mrs. Daley,

> *Enjoy the memories, but don't forget to look to the future. You are stronger than you think.*

> *Neil (The salvage guy)*

I don't care if I get cancer

"Your head looks like a fuzzy yellow duck, Grandma."

"Josh, come sit on my bed. You are the most handsome six-year-old in the whole world. The way you're growing, you'll probably be over six feet tall."

Josh hangs onto the gray metal doorframe at the entrance to Room 417. "Grandma, I want to go now. It smells funny in here, and I don't like all the wires on you."

"Just one hug before you go, sweetheart. That's what I miss the most. Those big bear hugs before you go to school."

"No, Grandma. No hugs." He turns and runs down the hospital hallway to the elevator.

Tears roll down Christine Baker's face. She has pancreatic cancer and is not expected to live.

"Don't be upset, Mrs. Baker," Nurse Raeburn says. "Cancer is frightening for children."

Christine turns blurry eyes toward the nurse. "Josh is my grandson. I've raised him from birth because my daughter has a drug problem. He's all I have left, and now I don't even know if he loves me."

On Friday evening, the nurse brings a phone to Christine's bed. It's Josh.

"Hello, Grandma."

"Thanks for calling me, sweetheart. Your smile was the first thing I thought of when I woke up today. I miss you so much. Are you happy at Auntie's?"

"Grandma, I don't like her potatoes. They have onions and green leaves in them. She never makes red Jell-O, and she says chocolate milk is bad for you. Sparky barks at her cats, and my bike has a flat front tire."

"She loves you, Josh. She's taking care of you while I'm sick, and she's doing her best. I'll give her my recipe for white sugar cookies with sprinkles."

"She probably won't make them. She says sugar makes me hyper."

There's an awkward silence.

"Is everything all right, Josh?"

She can hear him breathing into the phone. Finally, he speaks very softly. "My teacher got mad at me in front of the whole class today, Grandma."

"Why, sweetheart?"

"She asked me if my grandma was getting better. I told her you were almost dead. She pointed her finger at me and said never to say that about you. But it's true, isn't it, Grandma?"

"The angels are waiting for all of us, sweetheart. I'm not afraid of dying. When are you coming to see me again?"

"I don't want to come to that place anymore." He pauses, then asks, "Grandma, I'm afraid to go to bed. Can you sing me the song about the little calf?"

Christine struggles to sit upright and begins to sing softly into the phone. It's a song she made up and sang to him whenever he had trouble falling asleep. It's about a baby calf that's lost and afraid until it finally finds its mother.

Nurse Raeburn, who has just entered the room with another dose of pain medication, wipes her eyes as she waits for Christine to finish the song.

Two weeks later, on a Sunday morning, Christine is awakened by her grandson standing beside her hospital bed, wearing a crisp, white shirt.

"Josh, I've missed you so much."

He crawls up the shiny metal frame of the hospital bed and hugs her neck, not wanting to let go.

"Now I'm going to get cancer too, and then we'll both die and be together, right, Grandma?"

"What?"

Josh snuggles closer to his grandmother in her hospital bed. He looks up into her jaundiced face. "My friend Bethany told me her grandma had cancer and her auntie kept hugging her and then she got cancer too and both of them died. But I don't care anymore if I get cancer. I just love you so much, Grandma."

Desperate old man
hides out in grizzly country

The gray-haired woman riding the buckskin gelding pulls up short.

That shiny red nylon tent wasn't beside the creek yesterday. The campers must have showed up after sundown.

Thick smoke rises from a small campfire piled high with dead pine branches. An aluminum walking cane and a pink Winnie the Pooh umbrella rest against the front of the zippered tent. A flimsy green plastic table is covered with open cans, cereal boxes and a half-empty bag of marshmallows. A dirty brown VW is hidden under a large fir tree.

"Stupid to leave open food lying around," she thinks. "Bears could smell that miles away."

The Boyd Mountain area is government property, and the public are allowed to camp there temporarily, but it's been a long time since anybody has. Millie Bass is curious about who's set up next to her ranch and why.

She taps her buckskin's flank and heads down into the gully.

A thin, balding, sixty-something man in a wrinkled white dress shirt comes out of the tent holding a tiny blonde girl wrapped in a cheap yellow sleeping bag.

"Howdy," Millie calls to the startled campers. "You folks know where you are? There's grizzly around. Shouldn't be leaving food open like that."

The man stands and faces her defiantly, holding the toddler close to his chest. "We have a right to camp here. I checked with the government office."

She nudges her horse a few steps closer. "Just being neighborly."

The man looks up at the woman in the saddle and then limps towards her. The little girl clings shyly to his neck. Her left cheek is badly bruised.

Millie stiffens. "Who's the little girl? Did you do that to her?"

"No. And it's none of your business."

"Maybe it's police business."

"Rebecca's my granddaughter."

"Why'd you bring her way out here?"

"I'd rather take my chances with a grizzly bear than leave her with the man living in my daughter's house. I couldn't take her to my apartment. He knows where I live."

She nods. "Planning on staying long?"

"I don't know."

"You can't camp out here all winter. I've seen forty below. My name's Millie Bass. I own the ranch just up the road. Got plenty of room. You can stay as long as you like."

The man hesitates. "We'll stay here."

In the morning, when he crawls out of the tent, Rebecca's grandfather is startled to see a man sitting on the ridge above their tent. He has a large scorpion tattooed on his neck and a rifle across his knees.

"Who are you?"

"I'm Derek, one of Millie's ranch hands. She sent me here last night to keep an eye on you, watch for grizzlies." He pauses. "Millie invite you to stay at her place?"

The older man nods.

"If I were you, I'd take her up on it. Millie's rescued a lot of people." He looks down. "I'm one of them."

Within the hour, Rebecca and her grandfather are in the shiny pine kitchen at Millie's J-Bass Ranch.

Rebecca stares hungrily at the fluffy hotcakes rising on the griddle.

"Why do you do it?" the older man asks.

Millie gently touches the little girl's unwashed hair. "I was five. My mother's drunken boyfriend pulled me out of bed and threw me against the wall for leaving my dollhouse on the steps. Escaped as soon as I could, when I was fifteen. Came here. It's a safe place."

Rebecca's mother sobs with relief when she gets the phone call. "Thank you for keeping Becca safe, Dad. I love you."

Two months later, she arrives at the big log gate with all her belongings.

Calvin and Bunny in the big city

"We'll never make it, Bunny. You'll be late."

Calvin tries to squeeze his old truck and camper around the stalled plumbing van. They're trapped on the bridge leading into the city. His wife's first chemotherapy treatment starts in fifteen minutes.

Calvin and Bunny Keller started out yesterday. It's a ten-hour drive. The mountain scenery was breathtaking. They talked about their lives together, their children and grandchildren, their log home and her favorite palomino mare.

They slept in their homemade camper and watched the sun come up over White Eagle Lake. There should have been plenty of time to get downtown by 8:45.

Now they're stuck in traffic. "I forgot about Monday morning rush hour, honey. I'm sorry."

Bunny's worried about the chemo, even though she doesn't say much. Calvin feels guilty for misjudging the time.

Finally, a tow truck arrives and picks up the van in front of them. They're crawling along again, bumper to bumper.

Rutherford Regional Cancer Center is on 41st Avenue. There's underground parking next door, but their crew cab truck and camper won't fit. Two blocks away, he finds an open lot.

They need two spaces for their old brown Ford with its yellow wooden camper. It looks out of place here.

Calvin says, "Get your things out of the camper, honey. I'll get us a ticket."

The ticket machine stands under a red-and-white sign: "Valid tickets must be displayed. Violators will be towed IMMEDIATELY at owner's expense. Cars towed $125. Trucks towed $175. Storage $25 per day. Agostino Towing. 722-555-3000."

The machine looks complicated, a line of mystery buttons with scrolling digital directions on a tiny screen. "Daily rate $12.00. Exact change or credit card." He has $3.15 in change and no credit card.

"Got any change, Bunny?"

"Sorry, dear," she replies. "I used my last couple of dollars to buy those snacks last night."

Calvin searches under the seats for coins. Sixty-five cents and a few shell casings from his hunting trips. "Never mind," he says. "I'll get change and pay on the way out."

Calvin takes his wife's hand. As they start down the street, he looks back to see the flashing yellow lights of a tow truck entering the parking lot. His heart sinks.

They enter the cancer clinic an hour late.

"Good morning, folks," the nurse says. "We're behind schedule so we'll start right away. Please stay with your wife, Mr. Keller."

Near supper time, Bunny's treatment is finally over. She's exhausted. She waits in a wheelchair as Calvin walks back to the parking lot. He's not hopeful that the truck will still be there.

What will he tell Bunny?

But the truck and camper are still there! There's a note on the bug-splattered windshield: "I was here when you tried to buy a ticket. I guessed you were going to the Rutherford Center. Your parking fee is on me today."

As Calvin pulls out, the tow truck pulls in. The driver waves him over.

"It's your lucky day, buddy. I was gonna yank your hunk o' junk, but some guy bought a ticket for you. Your over-sized rig would have paid me a couple hundred bucks today."

"Who was he?" Calvin asks.

"Don't know. Some big shot in a Lexus. Got his suit dirty puttin' a note on your windshield."

The tow truck driver shakes his head. "I still can't believe it. As the rich guy was leavin', I asked him: 'Why you botherin' with them hillbillies?' He looked me square in the eye and said, 'My daddy drove a truck like that.'"

I would be happy
for the rest of my life

Danielle opens her grandmother's freezer looking for ice cream. She's horrified to find it stuffed with supermarket flyers, old clothes, an alarm clock and two crushed lampshades.

She's come from her office to join them for lunch.

Grandpa Joe and Grandma Bitsy are at the round oak table by the kitchen window. There are blue-and-white soup bowls on the barn-scene placemats she remembers from her childhood.

Grandma is quiet today, staring at the clock on the wall.

Would you like some apple pie, Grandma? Baked fresh this morning by Sundstrom's Bakery..."

"No, I'm sick of all this pie! Just leave us alone!"

A few minutes later in the living room, Grandpa explains. "Grandma didn't mean it, sweetheart. She didn't sleep well last night."

"Grandpa, you haven't been truthful. You said she was OK, that it was just the new medication. She's sick, isn't she?"

Birgitta "Bitsy" Bennett is seventy-three. Swedish-born, she still speaks with a slight accent. Bitsy met Joe Bennett on a college ski trip fifty-one years ago and married him three months later.

They've had a wonderful life together—four children, ten grandchildren. And scores of grateful students from her decades of teaching school.

Joe is as much in love with her today as when he laced up her boots at the Blue Pine Ski Lodge.

Grandpa insists, "Our doctor is working on some different medications. Don't worry, Danielle. She's going to be just fine."

Joe Bennett is doing his best to keep his wedding vows, trying to "accept the unacceptable." As he dries the dishes, he thinks, "We're all a bit forgetful. Who wouldn't get cranky once in a while when your back aches and your ears aren't as sharp as they used to be?"

Weeks go by. Joe keeps busy around the yard. Bitsy watches from the kitchen window.

He realizes the house needs some modifications. There's a Home Depot just down the street. A friendly fellow in an orange apron takes the list and locates what Joe needs. "Why do you need locks for the tops of your doors?" he asks. "Are you worried about break-ins?"

Without warning, all of Joe's pent-up feelings spill out in aisle four of the Home Depot. "I don't want to do it, but I can't sleep anymore with my wife wandering like she does. Last night, I found her rummaging through our neighbor's mailbox."

Joe breaks down, wracked with emotion. "Most of the time, she doesn't even know who I am. She calls me Bjorn. I don't even know anyone by that name."

Steve leads him to a back room. Within twenty minutes, Danielle is there to pick him up. He finally admits to Bitsy's "illness of forgetfulness."

The Bennett family make arrangements, and Bitsy is moved to a room in the memory care wing of the Bayshores Retirement Community.

All her favorite things go with her: the blue-and-white gingham curtains, the round oak table with the barn-scene placemats, the family photos from the dining room wall.

Joe can't imagine sleeping alone and asks to stay with her the first night.

As he turns down her bed, Bitsy touches his hand. "Are you married, Bjorn?"

"Yes, I am," he replies. "I've been married to a beautiful, blue-eyed Swedish gal for over fifty years."

"Oh, that's too bad, Bjorn. If you weren't married, I'd marry you myself. You're so kind, and handsome, too. I would be happy for the rest of my life if I was married to a wonderful man like you."

The man who played everyone's piano

"It's time for you to leave. You have absolutely no intention of buying this piano, do you?"

The stylish, middle-aged woman starts to pull down the keyboard lid while the unkempt man continues to play.

His long fingers are strong and sure on the keys. His scuffed green bowling shoes work the pedals with ease. He continually shakes his head to the side to keep a shock of stringy gray hair out of his eyes. His stained and wrinkled blue cowboy shirt is missing a pocket snap.

"I've always appreciated the tone of a Steinway, ma'am. I'm moving to an apartment in the summer. That's why I'm looking around."

Jasper Janowski, fifty-two, is a piano junkie. New music comes into his head every day, amazing compositions, full and rich, like Gershwin. If he doesn't get a chance to actually hear them with his ears, he is likely to go mad.

Neither Jasper nor anyone in his family has ever owned a piano. He learned to play in department stores, music stores and church basements. He's on call as a laborer with a piano mover. Fifteen bucks a move and one hour free on whatever piano is in their warehouse at the time.

Music store managers have banned him because sales activity stops when he plays. The manager of Manhattan Music declares: "This is a music store, not a free concert hall."

If you ask his Aunt Agatha, she will tell you that he's always been strung a little differently. But then she'll look away and smile, "That kid still makes me cry when he plays."

Jasper has done his best to fight the addiction, sometimes going up to a week without touching the ivories, but it's no use. His ten fingers are slaves to the eighty-eight keys.

Today, he's answered a classified ad: "1928 Steinway grand. Refinished rosewood, new strings, pin block and dampers. Original ivories. $58,000 obo."

The Tudor-style house is in an upscale neighborhood.

He has eleven dolllars in his pocket and no bank account.

As he plays, a raspy voice calls from down the hall. "Turn off that infernal stereo! I told you never to play Oscar Peterson's music again! It reminds me too much of..."

The woman steps back submissively from the piano as an angular man in a blue suede jacket comes into the room. He is somewhat past middle age with graying hair.

"Ben," she stammers. "I'm sorry..."

Oblivious to the second person in the room, Jasper plays on. The older man stands mesmerized.

Ben Starks is an agent. Within a week, he has signed Jasper Janowski to a complicated contract that Jasper hasn't bothered to read. The "unlimited use of a piano" clause is all Ben's new client cares about.

Jasper's new stage name is "JJ Jagger." Although looking out of place in a tux and tails, he is soon playing in clubs. A concert tour is planned, and time has been booked in a recording studio.

Five years later, Jasper is widely recognized as one of the country's great jazz artists. His compositions go platinum, and his concerts are sold out, but the rights to his music—past, present and future—are controlled by his agent. A fortune in royalties flows into the agency bank account. Jasper still gets barely enough to pay the rent on his apartment.

An entertainment reporter is writing a column on the rumored injustice of Jasper's contract. He corners Jasper in the hall after a concert. "How do you feel about the way Ben Starks has manipulated your contract?"

Jasper's face breaks into a wide smile. "I'm very grateful to Mr. Starks! He kept his promise. Now I get to play every day without fail."

Nobody stands

"Must you park that bug-spattered contraption right in front of my house? I'm sure the neighbors don't appreciate having their views blocked every time you visit me."

Monty Kaplan, thirty-five, is a trucker, hauling industrial glass across the country.

His mother, Patricia Kaplan, is profoundly disappointed. She wanted the finer things in life for her son Montgomery, whom she adopted at birth. She started him off in classical piano lessons at age five, hoping he would follow a lifetime path of cultured learning.

Monty found the lessons difficult. "My fingers hurt from those hard scales, Mother. I can't remember all those notes. I want to ride my bike with Mario."

But Patricia persisted, and Monty continued with his lessons until age fourteen. He studied all styles: baroque, classical, romantic and contemporary. He played recitals and bowed courteously while receiving polite applause from crowds in black-and-white formal wear.

Then, one month after his fifteenth birthday, he disappeared into the basement with a scratched red guitar he'd found at a thrift store.

He never returned to the piano.

"That is a coarse instrument, Montgomery," his mother would shout down the stairs. "I'll not have the atmosphere of my home ruined with such vulgar attempts at music."

At sixteen, he left the tensions of home. "I love you, Mom, but it's time for me to go."

She didn't protest his leaving or offer any further support even though he hadn't finished high school.

Monty became a drifter, moving from job to job. After a few years, he found his niche in long-haul trucking.

The solitude of the open road fed his desire to write music of his own. When a tune came into his head, he would pull over, grab his old guitar and listen in wonder as new songs were born in the cab of his truck.

For years, his mother described Monty to her friends at the club as "trying to find himself." Eventually, she only referred to him as her "adopted son with problems."

Monty comes home every year for his mother's birthday. Unashamedly, he parks his aging Peterbilt in front of her house and brings in a bouquet of roses and a card from a gas station. The writing in the card is always the same. "Happy Birthday, Mom. Thank you for raising me."

Patricia is always polite but lukewarm when her son arrives. "Will you stay for tea before you get on with hauling whatever it is you are hauling?"

At the kitchen table, Monty pulls out a crumpled brown envelope filled with homemade CDs, along with hamburger wrappers and torn paper napkins with lyrics and music scribbled on them. "I'm writing my own songs now. I'm talking to a record company. The guys at the truck stops keep asking for more of the CDs I make on my computer."

His mother begins to weep. "Where did I go wrong in raising you, Montgomery? Why did you choose such a mindless profession when you could have been on the world stage?"

She rushes to her bedroom. She hears the diesel engine start up.

Six months later, Monty is killed, crushed by a falling wall of glass while loading his rig.

One year after his death, the number one song on the country charts is titled "Am I a Stranger?" Music and lyrics by Monty Kaplan.

Later that year, when receiving the award for single of the year, the female singer who recorded his song says to the audience, "The man's lyrics never fail to touch me. I never met him, but he must have had an incredible relationship with a woman."

She shades her eyes and looks out over the audience. "Is there anyone here from his family?"

Nobody stands.

Holdup at Flip-n-Phil's

"One double-egger and a small orange juice," echoes the teenaged girl wearing the headset. "That will be five dollars and fifty-seven cents."

The green station wagon with faded wood trim sputters its way toward the cashier's window, blue smoke puffing from its wobbly exhaust pipe. It travels a full car length past the window before stopping, its brakes squealing horribly.

The driver, an older woman with huge wraparound sunglasses and auburn-tinted hair, gets out of the car and walks back to the "pay" window. She is wearing a maroon silk dress with a gaudy, gold-colored brooch.

The woman leans her head in the window as it slides open. "I'm very sorry, young lady, but I've just discovered that I've forgotten my pocketbook this morning. If you'll just give me a moment, I will search for the emergency cash I keep hidden in my car for times like this.

The cashier smiles politely. "I'm sorry, but you can't do that. If you would just pull ahead and park in stall number 3A..."

The old woman hasn't heard her. She is walking back to her car, waving a white handkerchief weakly to the drivers waiting behind her. Then she swings open the back door and lifts up the floor mats.

It's 8:00 a.m., and the drive-through line at Flip-n-Phil's Restaurant is now stretching well into the parking lot.

A young mother in a white minivan begins to honk. The driver of a black BMW, second in line, inches backward, trying to stay out of the puffs of smoke now building into a hazy cloud around the gigantic old wagon.

Another horn blows relentlessly as the older lady stretches over the back seat, feeling into the side storage pockets of the rear luggage area.

An impatient man in a pin-striped suit gets out of his silver Nissan and begins shouting at her. "We call this a 'drive-through,' lady, not a 'drive-in.' If you don't have the money, stay home!"

She can't hear him above the burbling of her car's muffler.

His irritation bubbling over, the man rushes up to the cashier's window. "I absolutely can't wait any longer for some old lady with no money!"

The cashier calls as loudly as she can and finally gets the old lady's attention. "Ma'am, please pull ahead and park in stall number 3A. I'll hold your order while you look. Ask for Bridget when you come inside."

The old lady looks up, flustered, her right hand clenched in a tight fist. She shuffles over to the driver's door and gets behind the wheel. She manages to urge the sputtering wagon several yards forward and get it halfway into the parking space before it backfires and stalls in a cloud of blue smoke. She gets out and walks quickly inside the restaurant without looking back.

The horns stop blowing, and the line of cars moves forward.

Inside the restaurant, the older woman moves to the far end of the counter near the drive-through window. "Bridget, please," she calls urgently.

Bridget motions for the driver in the black BMW to wait, then turns and steps quickly towards her. "Did you find your money?" she asks.

The woman holds out a handful of crumpled hundred-dollar bills and says sweetly, "Please allow me to pay for everyone's order until I tell you to stop. I like to treat people when I can, and I don't often get the chance these days. I've annoyed some of these busy folks with my forgetfulness this morning."

"It's very kind of you to offer, but you can't afford to pay for other people's orders," says Bridget.

"Don't worry, sweetheart," says the lady, gently touching her large gold brooch. "My dear George left me more than enough."

I'm giving you my baby

Trevor Chapman pulls his Volvo wagon off the freeway into a busy rest area.

They've only been on the road forty minutes, and already his wife Carrie and ten-year-old son Eric need to stop.

He's patient. It's family vacation time.

While waiting in the car, he searches for his favorite music channel.

A teenage girl approaches the passenger door and taps on the glass. Her face is half-covered, dark eyes filled with tears. She's holding a bundle wrapped in a thick, white towel.

Trevor reads her lips through the glass: "I need help." He opens the door.

She lays the bundle on the passenger seat, places her backpack on the floor beside it and in a quiet voice says, "I'm giving you my baby. Her name is Vinita. She's three days old."

Before he can speak, she closes the door and, without looking back, runs into the woods behind the rest stop.

Carrie returns to find her husband holding a newborn baby and pointing to the trees. "A girl just gave me her baby and ran away. What do we do now?"

Carrie is calm. "Give me the baby, Trevor. Look in the backpack. Maybe we can find out who she is."

The backpack contains diapers, formula, bottles and a sealed white envelope. Trevor tears it open. She's written with a red pen on yellow, lined paper:

Parents of my baby,

I came here today looking for the right family. I choose you. I can't give Vinita the life she deserves. In my culture, what I have done brings horrible shame to my family. I cannot tell them about my baby. Her father is not of my race.

Please care for her like I wish I could.

Please teach her to play the piano when she is older. It is very important to me.

I will love her with all my heart, until my very last breath.

Trevor takes a deep breath and reaches for his phone.

Eric reaches over and touches the baby's tiny fingers. "Can we keep her, Dad?"

Trevor glances at Carrie. For years, they have prayed that God would give them a daughter, the natural way.

"No, son. She's been abandoned. We've got to call the authorities."

Quickly Trevor dials 911, afraid of being suspected of child abduction.

A local police officer and two women from Children's Services arrive in twenty minutes. They assure the Chapmans they've done the right thing. Baby Vinita is taken into the custody of the state, classified as "abandoned."

Carrie Chapman is shaking. "What will happen to her now?"

As the social worker wraps the baby in a clean, pink blanket, she replies: "After a hospital check, she'll go to a foster home for the waiting period. Then, she'll be eligible for adoption. If her mother comes back in time, she still has the right to apply for custody."

The police officer shakes Trevor's hand. "Thanks, folks, for being good citizens. If you hadn't been here, the mother might have just abandoned her baby in the woods."

Their vacation is the worst ever. Everyone's edgy. Was Vinita really destined to be theirs?

On the way back, forty minutes from home, Trevor exits the freeway. He drives directly to the Children's Services office, then to the local village newspaper, where he inserts this notice into the classifieds:

To Vinita's mother:

We have decided to accept your precious gift. We are applying to adopt her. If we are successful, you can be sure we will protect her and love her as our own. You would be welcome to visit her. Contact us confidentially at Box 367, this paper.

P.S. Our great aunt has offered us her white baby grand piano for Vinita.

Pour in new blood

Alf Weaver raises his shovel and takes a vicious swing at the offender.

The shaggy sheep dog yelps and scurries across the narrow country road, dragging its left hind leg.

Alf's fifteen-year-old grandson Shane runs across the field toward him. "What was that for?"

"Stupid mutt was digging up my watermelon vines."

"That's no reason to beat him! Digging's what dogs do, Grandpa."

"Not in my garden, they don't. No critter's gonna wreck my stuff and walk away healthy."

"You just did it because you're mean! I'm telling the neighbors what you did."

"If they ask, I'll tell them the mutt got hit by a truck. And you'll tell them the same thing."

"I'm not going to lie for you, Grandpa. I'm going to tell them the truth."

"You'll tell them what I tell you to tell them, or you'll be out on your ear, young man. Respect your elders."

Shane and his mother live with his grandfather because they have no other place to go. Shane's mother has emotional problems and spends most of her time watching soaps in her bedroom.

Alf Weaver is a stocky, bald, angry man with watery, gray-blue eyes. He constantly criticizes everyone in the house for being untidy. He calls Shane a sneaky little thief, and he belittles his daughter-in-law for being fat.

Shane turns and runs into the woods on the other side of the creek.

"Run away, you little coward! You're a worthless piece of trash, just like your father! You'll never be any better than him."

Shane pushes his face against the rough bark of a cedar tree and screams: "Why do I have to have that man's blood in me? Why can't the doctor drain it all out and pour in new blood? Why can't I have a good family?"

That evening, when Shane finally returns home, his grandfather is in the kitchen. He looks up from the massive plate of spaghetti and meatballs he's shoveling into his mouth and growls, "I've already been to the neighbors, so don't bother yapping to them about the dog."

Shane stands squarely in the doorway. "I may have some of your blood running through me, but I'm never going to be like you. I'm not going to be mean or tell lies or hurt people. After what you did today, I've decided that we aren't going to live here anymore. Mom and I are leaving."

Alf smirks. "Where you goin'? Neither of you got a dime."

"I called that women's shelter we went to when we had the trouble with Dad. They said we can stay there for at least a few days. After that, I don't know. But anything's better than here. I may have your name, but I'm not the same inside."

Somewhere in his walk in the woods, Shane seems to have crossed the invisible line from boyhood to manhood.

His grandfather's eyes darken. "I told the neighbors what happened to their dog," he says and pauses. "They said they could understood why you chased it out of our garden and said it wasn't your fault it got winged by the truck. Stupid dog's worthless anyhow. Drags everybody's garbage around."

Shane's face hardens. "On my way back to the house, I filled in the hole by the watermelons."

He drops something on the table. "This was lying at the bottom."

It's a tarnished gold pocket watch with the initials A.W. engraved on the back. "That 'stupid' dog's digging found the watch you blamed me for taking. Looks like you dropped something, Grandpa."

I'll tell you a picture

"Lady, you're in the men's room. Can't you read?"

To her horror, Doris looks up from washing her hands and realizes there's a man behind her.

With her head down, she rushes from the restroom into the mall, searching for her daughter.

"Mother, what's wrong?" Her daughter grasps her shoulders.

"I've never been so humiliated. I just used the wrong restroom. I'm never coming to this mall again as long as I live."

Doris Dawson is losing her sight but doesn't want to admit it. There's a dark patch in the center of her vision.

"Mother, maybe it's time for new glasses. You need a style change anyway."

Doris tries to convince herself that new glasses are the answer and promises to get her eyes checked soon.

Three days later, Doris walks into an advertising sandwich board in front of a restaurant. The falling sign hits a white poodle being walked by an older gentleman. The yelping draws a crowd, and again she leaves the scene in embarrassment.

At the end of the week, her eye doctor gives her the life-changing news. "Doris, you're losing your sight rapidly. You are already legally blind and can expect total sight loss within several years. I will help you through the process. Many of my patients still enjoy a fine quality of life."

At home in her favorite green chair by the window, she asks hard questions: "Did I read too much at night? Should I have bought better glasses? Is it because I looked directly at the sun for a few seconds during the solar eclipse when my brother dared me to? Why me? Will I be able to remember what all the colors look like when everything is black?"

*****

Tap. Tap. Tap.

Two years later, Doris has to feel for the curb with her long, white cane. She's totally blind.

Her family have learned to adapt. Blind etiquette teaches rules such as "Please don't leave the room without telling me." (People who are blind often find themselves talking to thin air.)

A new family moves in next door, and, unexpectedly, the eleven-year-old daughter, Hannah, takes a special interest in Doris. They become friends.

Hannah describes herself as tall with long, brown hair and dark eyes. She speaks with an unusual accent and sometimes seems to be absent-minded, but Doris loves her company and enjoys the hours Hannah spends reading to her on the back patio.

Doris asks her, "Why would you want to spend your time with a woman who is blind? Don't you have lots of younger friends?"

Hannah replies, "You're a good friend. That's better."

On Saturdays, Hannah takes Doris for walks. Her favorite saying is, "I'll tell you a picture, Mrs. Dawson."

The traffic is rushing by. Hannah stops by a wrought-iron gate next to a Chinese restaurant and describes the "city garden" someone has created. Doris remembers it vaguely from when she was sighted, but she had never taken much notice of it as she had hurried by on her way to the bank.

"There are red pots and yellow flowers. Water is running into a shiny, green dish and back out again. A striped, orange cat is sleeping on a wooden chair."

As Doris is enjoying the word pictures, truck tires screech directly behind them. Startled, she grabs for Hannah's arm. Hannah continues describing the scene, undisturbed.

At that moment, Doris understands. Hannah's unusual speech is a deaf accent.

She fumbles for her young friend, finds her face and turns it toward her.

"You can't hear me, can you?"

"Mrs. Dawson, you are my friend. I can see you. That's good enough."

Ready to make millions

"Say it out loud. Let your subconscious mind hear it in your own voice."

Hundreds of seminar attendees chant out the slogan being flashed on the screen at the front of the hotel meeting room: "I have unlimited potential."

Marty, near the end of the fifth row, repeats the words quietly at first, then louder.

The screen image changes. A young father is steadying the back of a child's bike. The child's scuffed running shoes are dug into the pavement, resisting.

The new chant begins: "I've been held back too long by fear of failure."

Marty closes his eyes and repeats the words. That's him. At thirty-seven, he feels like a loser, living paycheck to paycheck, buying lotto tickets and hoping for a big break.

While others are making their mark, he's making payments on a middle-class bungalow and a three-year-old minivan. His wife and kids feel his constant restlessness.

He's driven fifty miles to attend this one-day, life-changing seminar. A two-hundred-dollar credit card charge has bought him a coil-bound workbook, a ticket for a "power nutrition" luncheon and an envelope of discount coupons for books stacked on folding tables next to the exit doors.

The keynote speaker is a pro football player who broke his back, then changed his focus and went on to make millions on the speaking circuit.

Marty's looking for someone to inspire him. A mentor. Someone with "life credentials."

The image on the screen changes again: a well-dressed couple in a white Mercedes passing through the electronic security gate of their Mediterranean villa. A prompt line flashes: "I am financially successful."

Marty can't repeat those words. He's not financially successful. That's why he's here.

An assistant notices that he's fallen silent and moves in. She glances at his name tag, puts her arm around him and speaks directly into his ear, "Marty, verbalize this three times a day, and it will come true. We have personal success stories in our brochure that prove it."

He nods, really wanting to believe.

To a background of rock music pounding out of ceiling speakers, the tanned keynote speaker bounces onto the stage wearing an open-necked designer shirt and three strands of gold chain. He waves his hand over the audience. "Are you ready to change your life today? Are you ready to make millions?"

Marty glances at those around him, dressed in new clothes bought at discount stores for the occasion. They're all standing, fists of determination in the air, shouting, "Yes! Yes! I will make millions."

Like him, these people are desperately hoping that the man on stage can give them the successful life they've always wanted, that he will make them millionaires just as he has the thousands of other people who have attended his seminars over the last five years.

Inside Marty's head, emergency warning lights are flashing. He slides to the aisle and bolts out the side door. He closes his eyes and breathes deeply.

"Can helped you, sir?"

Marty opens his eyes. He is in the corridor of the food service area, face to face with a startled immigrant worker carrying a yellow plastic bin overflowing with vegetable peelings.

"Where's the nearest exit?" he asks anxiously.

"No understand exit," the worker replies with a broad smile. "You need chicken sandwich?"

Marty stares straight into the immigrant worker's eyes. "Are you happy?"

The worker grins. "Yes, yes, my life bery good. Work hard. Send money my family. Someday, all come live me here."

Marty grabs his hand and shakes it, then follows the corridor to the lobby.

He calls his wife from a payphone. "Sweetheart, I'll be home early."

She asks wearily, "Did you find the seminar helpful?"

"Let's just say I met a man today who truly inspired me. It's the shot I needed!"

I'm Tabatha
when she's mad

"You've turned my house into a filthy, disgusting pigpen."

The elderly woman on the porch grasps the doorframe and glares at the younger woman standing inside. The room behind her is thick with cigarette smoke.

"I don't know who you are, lady, but you're not my landlord. I pay my rent to Victor, and I'm only two weeks behind, so get off my porch." The young woman slams the door in her face.

Edith Shipley turns and starts down the steps.

Six months ago, she sold her home to a developer.

It broke her heart to leave the white, stucco bungalow her husband built for her. He paid for the land by working part time as a night watchman. He mixed the cement for the foundation by hand. This was their first and only home. Her daughters' lives were formed here.

But when the developer's front man came to her door with a brown leather briefcase, she knew she had no choice.

He explained. "We've purchased twelve homes on your street already. There will be an industrial complex here. We'll pay you fair market value for your home and rent it out until we're ready to start construction. Then, it will be demolished.

She lives in a seniors' complex now, but still dreams about her old home. The peach tree by the back clothesline. The cedar porch swing that Otis built. She wonders about the family living there now.

This morning, Edith has returned to the house to see for herself.

It is a mistake.

The yard is waist-high with weeds. The front window is boarded up with a crooked chunk of stained plywood.

After the door is slammed in her face, Edith returns slowly and painfully to her pampered fifteen-year-old Chrysler.

As she looks back, a little girl with ginger hair steps onto the porch, clutching a ragged red flannel blanket and eating strawberry jam out of a can with her fingers.

Edith turns back. "What's your name, sweetheart?"

The child responds quietly. "Tabby, but my mommy calls me Tabatha when she's mad."

Edith makes her way back to the porch. As she approaches, Tabby coughs deeply. Her chest wheezes with each breath.

"What about your daddy?"

"Mommy says she hopes he never gets out of jail."

Edith sits heavily on the porch steps, weeping into her hands.

She feels a touch on her shoulder. The little girl with sad, green eyes and straggly, ginger hair sits right beside her. She whispers, "It's OK to cry, lady. My mommy cries all the time."

Edith pulls herself up. When the door opens again, she says gently to the young mother, "I'm sorry for what I said earlier. I lived in this house for almost fifty years, and I…" She searches for words. "I wonder if I could have a few peaches from the old tree?"

The young woman shrugs. "They'll just rot on the ground anyway."

Two days later, Edith is back, bringing a fresh, lattice-top peach pie. She learns that Tabby's mother goes by the name Susan Dunbar.

Over the next two years, they develop an uneasy relationship.

Finally, it's time for the old house to be demolished.

Susan's possessions are piled on the porch. Everyone is seated on blue, plastic milk crates around a battered kitchen table.

Tabby touches Edith's hand and says, "Look, Grandma-lady, I drawed a picture of you and a yummy peach pie."

Edith brushes a straggly lock of ginger hair from the child's face and then pulls her close.

Susan leans back and draws on a cigarette. "I'm gonna miss this place," she says unexpectedly. "I've been thinking. It's the best home I ever had, thanks to you."

An imperfectly discerned destiny

Troy Hamilton is a thirty-eight-year-old fast talker with no plans to get married.

Many matchmakers have schemed and failed. Dozens of women have set their scented traps, but he has sidestepped them all.

Acquaintances pepper him with questions: "Why are you afraid to get married? How do you cope with the loneliness?"

Troy shrugs. "I keep busy. I've got lots of friends."

Troy is an auctioneer. Sales records show he's a crowd favorite.

Sylvia Phillips, a local librarian, bought a small antique table at the auction last Thursday and fell in love. She's mesmerized by his amazing voice, his dreamy blue eyes and the way he looked at her when he said, "Sold to the pretty lady in the dark green coat!"

At thirty-four, Sylvia's biological clock is racing. Though not desperate, she's very interested in finding a good man.

Troy Hamilton is sure to be a good man.

She must find a way to meet him.

Next Thursday, she arrives an hour before the sale. "Is last week's auctioneer here? I have some questions for him about a table I bought."

Clever.

In a few minutes, Troy appears. He smiles and offers her his hand. "I remember you. That little antique table was a classic." He's obviously busy, but takes time to chat.

His eyes distract her. She gets flustered, forgets the made-up question she's planned and blurts out: "Does your wife like antiques as much as I do?"

Now, where did that come from? Her face is flushed, and her eyes fall to the floor.

Troy is quick to reply, "I'm single, never married. I love antique furniture. My house is full of it. I'd be happy to answer more questions after the sale, but right now I'm very busy."

Embarrassed, Sylvia leaves by a side door.

All week, she can't get him out of her mind. Next Thursday, she arrives late. When the auction's over, she goes looking for Troy, her usual shyness forgotten.

"Can we go for a coffee? I want to talk to you about antiques."

The office staff roll their eyes. Politely, he turns her down.

She tries several different tactics over the next few weeks, but nothing works.

She questions herself. "What's wrong with me?"

Her questions are answered later at the library. Troy doesn't know she works there. He checks out five books from the medical section. Sylvia looks up the titles after he's gone.

Troy Hamilton has inherited an untreatable disease. He's genetically marked for an early death. By staying single, he might have saved a woman from early widowhood.

Sylvia doesn't care. She confronts him with what she knows and what she feels.

Four months later, she marries a dying man. His blue eyes fill with tears as she promises to be there for him in sickness and in health: "Marriage is an unconditional commitment, a leap of faith into an imperfectly discerned destiny, an opportunity to love in the present, whatever the future might bring."

*****

The memorial service is a celebration of love. Troy's father weeps openly as he reads the eulogy. "For five glorious years, Troy and Sylvia had one of the most loving, happy marriages I have ever seen. If they had had their wish, they would have had many more wonderful years and grown old together. But it was not to be. None of us could have foreseen the carelessness of a drunk driver, the tragic automobile accident that claimed their lives. All of us can be comforted with the thought that they died instantly, with no pain, and they are together forever."

Screaming at the windshield

It's a typical street racer: purple Honda, lowered suspension, wing on the trunk, huge exhaust pipe. It's polluting the atmosphere with concussions of rap music from a pounding stereo.

Ted Bailey, driving a silver Lincoln, pulls up behind it, disgusted by the stupid cars some kids drive these days. "They're just out to kill themselves and anyone foolish enough to ride with them."

A blonde girl is in the passenger seat, not wearing a seatbelt. She turns sideways and waves to the red Corvette beside them. To his horror, it's Kerstin, his fifteen-year-old granddaughter.

The light turns green. Ted lays on his horn to get her attention. The tattooed teenage driver gives him a rude finger gesture and squeals across the intersection, changing lanes without signaling.

Ted punches the gas to keep up with him. The purple Honda easily outruns the Lincoln in the afternoon traffic, weaving in and out, its progress marked by a show of brake lights from startled drivers.

Within seconds, the Honda turns the wrong way down a one-way street, squeals around another corner and disappears.

Ted screams at the windshield, "I love you, Kerstin! Be safe, my angel, just be safe!"

His breath catches. "Not again!"

His hands are trembling on the wheel as he gives up the chase and pulls into a gas station.

Frantically, he dials her cell phone. No answer. She has a habit of forgetting to charge it.

He circles through the streets of the downtown core, hoping to catch sight of the car.

Impatient drivers honk and shake their fists at the gray-haired Lincoln driver, puttering along, scanning the traffic on a busy Friday afternoon.

Should he call his daughter and tell her that Kerstin is with some fool in a purple street racer?

How would that help? He was so upset with the guy's rude finger and the squealing tires that he didn't even get the license plate number.

He decides to wait in the mall parking lot at the end of her street. Ted Bailey tucks his Lincoln behind a supermarket sign and watches hopefully for the purple Honda.

Inevitably, his mind flashes back to another scene: a yellow Camaro upside down, the left front wheel still spinning, the irresponsible young driver struggling to free himself from the wreck, the still form of a blonde girl under crushed metal and shattered glass.

Ted's heart lurches with remembered grief and loss.

Two hours later, at 6:30 p.m., the Honda rumbles by and skids to a stop halfway down the block. Kerstin scrambles out and runs toward her house without looking back.

As Ted knocks on the door, he hears his daughter reprimanding Kerstin for being late, demanding to know where she's been.

He comes in casually, not wanting to let on that he knows about her wild ride.

"Hi, Grandpa." Kerstin smiles and hugs him. He has come just in time.

His daughter turns her attention from the scolding. "Hi, Dad. Nice of you to drop by. Can you stay for supper?"

After a tense meal with everyone picking at their food, Kerstin goes directly to her room. Ted makes his way upstairs and knocks gently on her door.

"I saw you in the purple car, sweetheart. I tried to catch up, but he was way too fast."

Kerstin shrugs. "We were just driving around. We didn't do anything. Nothing happened."

Ted sits down heavily on the bed. His face is ashen.

"Did I ever tell you that when I was seventeen, I used to drive a yellow Camaro?"

On behalf of the helpless

Bat Kruger is high on crack. Driving a stolen Ford diesel, a Glock semi-automatic pistol in his belt, he's invincible.

The pavement ends. The last streetlight shows a bumpy gravel drive to a farmhouse set well back from the road. The house is dark. A weak amber yard light, attached to the barn, blinks on and off behind a spreading red maple.

It's home invasion time. He'll get what he wants. They always listen when they're looking down the barrel of his Glock 357.

Bat kicks in the sidelight next to the front door, reaches around and unlocks the deadbolt. The hinges squeak, and he's inside.

Cordelia Cuthbert is startled awake at 1:30 a.m. by the sound of breaking glass. Heavy footsteps on the creaky basement stairs.

She's alone.

The old heating vent next to her bed looks directly into her basement. She spots the darting flashlight beam, hears doors slamming and smells a burning cigarette. Smoking has never been permitted in her home.

The intruder empties her freezer onto the concrete floor. He cracks open a cookie tin, stuffs his mouth with macaroons and heads back upstairs.

Cordelia is asthmatic. Her fear has triggered an attack. She's worried her wheezing will give away her presence.

Carefully, she removes a quilt from the cedar chest at the foot of her bed and tiptoes into the bathroom, silently closing and locking the door behind her.

The bathtub...he'll never look there. She conceals herself under the blue-and-white patchwork quilt. A hand towel stuffed in her mouth quiets her coughing.

As an afterthought, she removes her wedding ring and slips it under the fluffy white bath mat.

Bat is in the kitchen now, yanking drawers and dumping them. She hears silverware and china hitting the hardwood floor. He opens the fridge, chugs from a milk carton and throws it against the wall.

Next, Bat rips open the bifold doors on the coat closet. Cordelia hears the scrape of metal hangers on the rod as he systematically searches the pockets of every garment. Umbrellas from the top shelf clatter to the floor.

His boots thud in the hall. Frozen with terror, she couldn't scream if she tried. She tries to pray. The bouncing shafts of light under the bathroom door penetrate and violate her hiding place.

He tries the door. It's locked. A steel-toed boot strikes the handle, splintering wood, and now the flashlight beam is searching the bathroom. The flimsy white vinyl shower curtain tears off in his hand. Now the light shines directly on the unprotected lump of the patchwork quilt.

Bat jerks back a corner of the quilt. Cordelia looks up at a towering, faceless figure, obscured by shadows.

A few seconds of silence. Then, the intruder screams in terror. "Please...don't kill me!"

He turns and flees the room. A few long strides and he's back through the front door. Missing the first step off the front porch, he crashes to the ground.

Cordelia rushes to her bedroom window. She sees the invader bolting for his truck. The stolen diesel fires up, and dual wheels spray her front porch with gravel as he races down her driveway.

All is quiet. Her wheezing stops.

What did Bat Kruger see that night when he pulled back the blue-and-white patchwork quilt? A drug-induced hallucination? Some trick of shadow and light? A rare and unexpected intervention on behalf of the innocent and helpless?

Seven days
before the angels came

Rose Randall seems out of place on the park bench.

Walkers and joggers passing by are wearing casual clothes. She's dressed for dinner.

As a young mother approaches, pushing a stroller, Rose stands and motions her to stop.

"Can I push your baby?"

Startled by the unusual request, the mother angles the stroller to the opposite side of the path, takes several quick jogging steps and hurries away, looking back several times to see if the older woman is following her.

Rose watches until she disappears, then walks slowly across a grassy area towards a young family seated at a shiny cedar picnic table. She smiles and peers into the baby carrier on the bench beside the father.

"Can I hold your baby?"

The young father looks up from the watermelon he's eating. "Sure. His name is Timothy."

But Timothy's mother intervenes. "It's time for his bottle. Got to keep babies on schedule, you know." She grabs the carrier from beside her husband and places it on the table in front of her.

"Could I feed him then?" Rose asks.

"No. I'm sorry," the mother replies. "We need to get going." She signals her husband with a nod, and they begin to pack up.

Rose makes her way back to the gray concrete bench by the path.

Baby stores. Playgrounds. Most days, Rose can be found near infants and young children. She's often asked, "Are any of these your grandchildren?"

Childless, she's pursued a lifelong business career.

Her "Stella" line of women's evening wear is well known in exclusive stores. The direct, no-nonsense approach that served her so well in business seems to be inappropriate in the young parent community.

Who is this well-dressed older woman with the perfectly styled salt-and-pepper hair? Why does she want to touch their babies?

Rose lives alone in a rambling fieldstone house overlooking the bay. Her staff care for her peaceful Japanese gardens and prepare her meals.

No one visits. No one calls.

Who might let her hold or feed a baby or push one in a stroller? She doesn't appear to be the grandmother type. Her Louis Vuitton sunglasses are worth more than some of the family cars parked beside the playground.

Day after day, she hovers around mothers and young children. Day after day, she faces rejection and suspicion.

Before falling asleep each night, she remembers holding little Stella in the hospital. She was their miracle baby. Rose knew her for seven days before the angels came. Her husband Milton left a few months later. The business of dress design has successfully covered the pain in her life, until now.

On Saturday morning, Rose takes her place on a bench at the playground. Mothers whisper to each other and move away.

Within an hour, a parks department supervisor asks to speak with her. She follows him to a quiet spot by the maintenance building. "I'm sorry, ma'am, but people feel uncomfortable with you here. I must ask you not to approach the children."

Rose is shaken. With her head down, she walks slowly to her car.

Near the parking lot, she passes a young father with a baby in a canvas carrier against his chest. Tall and muscular, he seems agitated and is staring right at her. Is he one of the angry parents?

She looks the other way and keeps walking.

Unexpectedly, the young man calls after her. "Wait."

She stops and turns.

"I'm Darren. I've seen you here quite often. You always look so nice and friendly. Could you hold my baby while I use the restroom? I don't want to put her down on the floor in there. Her name is Ella. She'll smile for you."

Hating Daddy

"Mom, you can start buying baby clothes in blue. The ultrasound lady says she's ninety-nine per cent sure it's a boy. Brian and I decided to name him Anthony, after Dad."

"Jennifer, you can't do that. If you name your baby after your dad, I won't even be able to look at him. It will tear me up inside every time I say his name."

Kim Watson and her husband Tony divorced when their daughter Jennifer was three.

Five months ago, when Kim got the news she was going to be a grandmother, she blossomed. She showed up at Jennifer's apartment the next day with a gallon of yellow paint, ready to redecorate the second bedroom as a nursery. "Yellow is always safe. You can never be sure of what you're having until the baby's actually born."

After the ultrasound news, the issue of the baby's name comes up constantly between Jennifer and her mother.

Jennifer tells her, "When Dad was so sick at the end, I visited him every day. I know you hated him, but you could have at least showed up when he was dying."

Kim responds coldly, "All you ever saw of your father was the candy necklaces and the new pink bike and the trips to Sunshine Beach. Your father was a dreamer who couldn't keep a job. I had to raise you without any help from him. I stayed up nights when you could hardly breathe from the croup. I worked overtime to pay for your music lessons. Your father was never around for any of that. He only saw you when he wanted to."

"But he was still my father." Jennifer takes out a photo of her dad. "Just before he died, I asked him if I had a son, if he would like me to name the baby after him. He said that would be the best gift a father could ever receive. I'm giving him that gift, Mom. You're not going to stop me."

Kim heads for the door. "Naming your baby Anthony will be like sticking a knife in my heart. Is that what you want to do to your mother?"

When Jennifer goes into labor, Brian phones his mother-in-law from the hospital. Six hours later, the baby is born. Grandma hasn't come.

Brian calls Kim again and tells her that their baby looks a lot like her: molasses-colored eyes, button nose and thick, black hair.

Kim says nothing.

The baby goes home, but there is still no sign of the new grandmother. Is she really ready to disown her own grandchild because of the name?

Finally, the phone rings in Brian and Jennifer's apartment. Kim sounds tired and apologetic. "I've baked your favorite chicken tortellini casserole, sweetheart. Can I bring it over?"

"You've really hurt me, Mother, not being there when I had the baby. Did you hate Daddy that much?"

"You'll never know," Kim replies. "I lived with pain, anger and embarrassment every day since he left. He told everyone that no man on earth could live with a domineering woman like me and he was glad he got out. When he died of cancer, I honestly felt he was being punished for what he did to me."

"But, Mom, that's no reason to abandon me and the baby when we needed you this week."

"I haven't slept for days, Jennifer. It's been a terrible struggle. I finally realized I had to let go of my hate and anger. You can name the baby Anthony, and I will love him just as much."

"That's wonderful, Mom, but you don't have to call the baby Anthony. We named her Kimberly, after you."

Colton and the cart train

It's dusk. An amber light flashes as the shopping cart train snakes its way through the crowded parking lot near closing time.

It's the end of Colton's first day of work at Home Value Mart. The gangly eighteen-year-old is bringing in nearly a ton of wobbly-wheeled rolling stock gathered from all corners of the gigantic parking lot: twenty-seven shopping carts. Two stray carts were upside down in the shrubbery, but he straightened them out and got them lined up and rolling.

He needs this job badly because his mother has just lost hers.

His steps are unsure as he leads his train through the congestion. Steering the front cart with his right hand and clutching the "stop/start" control firmly in his left, he matches his pace to the speed of the self-propelled cart-mover pushing steadily from the back.

Colton is relieved as he rounds the final corner to the storage area at the front of the store.

A long, white Dodge van is parked near the front entrance with its back doors open. A muscular, middle-aged woman in a gray track suit is loading a stainless steel barbecue into the back.

Focused on his destination, he doesn't look back in time. The middle of his cart train grinds up against the van's back doors. He's misjudged the arc for the final turn.

She screams, "Stop the carts! I'm trapped!"

Colton drops the remote control and runs to her aid. He pulls desperately at the shopping carts, forgetting that the cart-mover with its amber flashing light is still forcing the cart train forward.

"I'll help you." Colton reaches for her hand across the tangled shopping carts.

"Just stop the carts, you idiot! Are you blind or stupid or both? You've wrecked my van, and you're crushing my legs!"

The storefront manager runs toward the scene. She grabs the remote and hits the stop button, releasing the pressure from the cart-mover. Then, she and Colton separate the carts and pull them away from the van.

Shaken and unsteady, Colton slips off his green Home Value Mart vest and hands it to the manager. "I know I'm fired. You don't have to pay me for today."

"Not so fast." The manager pulls out her notebook. "I need both of you to tell me what happened."

The customer is anxious to get going. She slams her damaged back doors shut and climbs into the driver's seat. "You'll hear from my lawyer in the morning."

The manager follows her to the driver's side window. "I'm very sorry, ma'am. I know you're upset, but I need some information before you leave. It's company policy. Could you give me your name and address?"

"No! Talk to my lawyer." She puts the van in gear.

The manager persists. "Our company pays for repairs and also gives our clients a thirty per cent discount on their purchases when unfortunate incidents like this happen. Can I please see your receipt for the barbecue?"

The woman blurts out, "I paid cash," steps on the gas and screeches out of the parking lot.

The manager becomes suspicious. A phone call to the police reveals the van is stolen. Within ten minutes, the police arrest Carlena Sophia Dodds, a thief with a lengthy criminal record. The stolen van and stainless steel barbecue are recovered.

Colton Wills becomes an unexpected hero. The local newspaper headline the next day reads: "Cart train driver traps barbecue thief."

His mother calls a friend across town. "Did you see Colton's picture on the front page? I'm so proud! You don't see many fearless young men like that anymore."

Not in the mood
for dying today

Stanley Murdoch is in bed seven of the Coronary Care Unit, dreaming about skating on Potter's Pond, when he is awakened by a commotion in the bed next to him.

"Can't you do something for him?" a dark-eyed young woman pleads. "He can't breathe."

The pale old man in the bed next to him is folded up in a blue hospital gown, gasping for air from the oxygen mask on his unshaven face.

Family members crowd around the bed as the doctor examines him. The women are weeping. The men stand quietly, with their arms folded.

The doctor directs their attention to the beeping heart monitor and shakes his head. He gently takes the oldest woman's hand.

"We'll keep him comfortable."

Within the hour, the curtain is drawn around bed six.

Stanley turns his head to the wall as they prepare fresh linens for the next patient.

He's not in the mood for dying today. Besides being hooked up to a mass of tubes and wires, he feels all right after his heart attack on Monday. He's just tired.

He hasn't realized he's drifted off until he feels his daughter's familiar touch on his shoulder.

"Good morning, Dad." Her face is beaming. "Michelle just had her baby. She's on the fourth floor. They'll bring her in to see you tomorrow. Such a little doll. Named after Mom."

"Are you sure they let newborns in here, honey?"

"Don't worry, Dad. The nurses know she's coming."

Family are welcome in the Coronary Care Unit. Occasionally, a child will visit, but never before have the staff seen a newborn on the ward.

Baby Emma is twenty-four hours old when she's introduced to her great-grandfather. Granddaughter Michelle places her against his chest, propped up with a hospital pillow.

Stanley traces the soft spot on her head with a twisted, arthritic finger and glances up at the family. "I hope you don't figure I'm strange, but I want to talk to her about a few things. I've been thinking all night about what to say."

Mother and grandmother sit and listen to a one-sided family conversation between a ninety-year-old and a one-day-old.

"Emma, I'm your great-grandfather. My old heart has beaten 3.5 billion times, your new one only about 150,000 times since you were born. I think mine's pretty well worn out. During the night when it's quiet, I feel it bumping away like an old John Deere tractor motor that needs oil."

A busy nurse steps up to his bed and hands the baby to Michelle. "This patient needs his IV adjusted." The nurse is unaware she's interrupting anything important.

With new tape on his wrist and all monitors checked, Stanley continues. "Emma, if I had more beats left, I'd take you to the fair to ride a Shetland pony. If I had more beats left, I'd buy you a red velvet dress for Christmas. If I had more beats left, I'd teach you to skate on Potter's Pond. I'd lace up your skates for you by the bonfire. That's where I kissed your great-grandmother for the first time."

Stanley strains against wires and tubes to sit up straight. A tear follows a crooked path down his weathered face.

Now he struggles with the words. "If I had more beats left, I could watch you grow up to be a loving, honorable woman like my first Emma."

He pauses. "But I'm glad I've had enough beats to hold you and tell you I love you. Since Monday, every beat has been a bonus beat."

At that moment, his heart monitor alarm rings. Staff respond to a "code blue" in bed seven. Within 1,000 beats, Stanley Murdoch leaves his second Emma to be with his first.

Percy the inventor

"Welcome to Sunnydale, Mr. Harris. You're in Room 213 with Mr. Bell. He's a retired plumber. Everybody likes him."

The cheerful care worker leads him to his room and opens the metal locker beside his bed. "Your clothes go in here. Supper's at five. Looks like chocolate cake for dessert tonight."

Percy Harris has been assessed with a type of dementia. His family is worried.

Quickly he scans the room. "Where will I hang my suit?"

She hesitates. "Everybody dresses casual here, Mr. Harris."

"But I'll need my blue suit for the meetings," Percy replies in an anxious tone. "I'm an inventor, you know."

"I'll wrap it in plastic and hang it behind the door for you."

He seems satisfied.

Percy is a stocky man with ice-blue eyes and a white brush-cut.

He's worked as a janitor for forty years but spent his free time chasing dreams and new ideas. Over the years, he's submitted twelve inventions to numerous agents, with no success. He's worked alone, afraid someone might steal his ideas.

His wife and daughter always knew when another invention was finished. Percy would slip on his navy blue suit and go downtown to meet "investors." When he returned, the story was always the same. "They're considering it seriously."

As Percy arranges his belongings, his new roommate shuffles through the door. "I'm Bill Bell. The last guy in that bed died last week."

Percy stands directly in front of him, feet wide apart, arms folded. "I'm Percy the inventor. I ain't ready to go yet. Got a dozen patents I'm marketing."

Soon, Room 213 looks like a high school science fair: flexible metal strips, molded plastic panels and multi-colored wires spread out on folding tables.

Bill's son, a successful businessman who visits every week, seems amused by their projects.

After a few weeks, the administrator comes by. She hovers at the door, watching the two men threading green and yellow wires through a small plastic box.

She clears her throat. "Gentlemen, your projects look very interesting, but you'll have to stop. Patient safety issues."

Percy throws up his hands. "But we're just ready to apply for a patent on the EZ-MedTrack. I think this one's gonna be big."

"I'm sorry, Mr. Harris, but I'm afraid you've run out of time."

Staff help them pack their inventions in a white cardboard box.

Over the next few months, Percy becomes withdrawn and uncommunicative. Soon, he quits speaking.

Bill the plumber passes away.

Two years later, Percy's wife receives an invitation for her and Percy to attend a special function at the care home.

As the evening begins, the administrator states, "We are here tonight to announce that a very significant donation is being made to Sunnydale by Mr. Scott Bell, president of Bell Industries."

The man everyone knows as "the plumber's son" takes the microphone. "Last week, my company received a patent for a wireless device that will revolutionize the way medications are monitored. In honor of my father, William Bell, I have decided to donate a portion of the profits to Sunnydale."

The administrator beams.

Scott continues. "I came across the early prototype for this device in a cardboard box that was given to me along with my father's effects after he died. I understand it was invented by my father and Mr. Percy Harris right here in Room 213. Therefore, I've also arranged for half the profits to go to the Harris family."

The crowd stands and applauds warmly. The administrator is speechless.

Percy's wife gently squeezes Percy's forearm.

He rises painfully from his wheelchair. Looking directly at the administrator, he says slowly, "Where did you hang my blue suit?"

Strangers at their wedding

The parking attendant is the first to know.

The lot is already full of beige Buicks and gray Chrysler sedans when the second wave hits.

From the driveway he calls the office. "They're parking in the fire lane, and a yellow Mustang convertible just backed over a row of marigolds."

Inside the chapel, college students and young couples with children search frantically for a seat amongst the dozens of gray heads. It will be standing room only.

Gradually the truth dawns. The Alderbrook Wedding Chapel has booked two ceremonies for exactly the same time.

Joel and Mandy are exchanging vows at 2:30, as are Orville and Ida. For Joel and Mandy, it will be for the first time. Orville and Ida are renewing theirs after sixty years together.

Mandy's aunt is weeping in the office of the chapel's wedding planner. "Mandy is like my daughter. I raised her from ten years old. How could you be so careless and ruin her wedding day like this?"

"I'm so sorry, ma'am. We just got a new computer system for bookings."

"You'd better get those old people out of there so Joel and Mandy can get married. I can't imagine Mandy sharing her wedding day with strangers who mean nothing to her."

The wedding planner calls the couples into her office and apologizes.

Joel makes a suggestion. "Let our minister marry us first. Then, if it's OK with the older folks, we'll stay up front and witness their recommitment. Although we didn't plan it this way, it may be a good start to our marriage."

The organist plays the wedding march. Joel and Mandy, both in their mid-twenties, make promises for life. Their pastor pronounces them husband and wife.

Orville and Ida's pastor leans on a shiny maple cane as he begins the second ceremony. "Dr. Schreiber, what have you to say to your bride?"

The elderly gentleman takes his wife's hand. "Ida, on another day, in another century, I stood with you before our family and friends. Once again, I take your hand as my life's partner. You are God's gift to me, my priceless treasure. I, Orville Schreiber, commit to you and you only for my lifetime."

At that moment, Mandy cries, "Dr. Schreiber!" She leaves her new husband's side, rushes to Orville, throws her arms around him and says boldly, "You delivered me!"

The audience gasps. Ida steps back. Joel steps forward and gently leads Mandy back to her spot on the platform.

The audience is more bewildered than ever.

After the ceremonies, the wedding planner apologizes again and explains her hastily revised plans for the photo sessions and reception rooms.

Mandy asks for the microphone. "I need to explain something. I'm sorry I interrupted Orville and Ida's ceremony. I was just so surprised to hear his name. I would have died at birth had it not been for Dr. Schreiber. My aunt told me the story. There was a terrible snowstorm, and the ambulance couldn't get through, but Dr. Schreiber risked his life, walking two miles down the train tracks to get to my mother."

Then Dr. Schreiber takes the microphone. "I remember that night well. The policy was to send out search and rescue volunteers on stormy nights, but Ida's feeling was very strong that I should go myself, and quickly. I arrived with only minutes to spare. This beautiful bride was the last baby I ever delivered."

Joel stands beside Orville. "Dr. Schreiber, when we come back from our honeymoon can you and Mrs. Schreiber teach us how to be married? I watched the way you kissed her after all these years."

Orville glances at his wife. "Well, Ida?"

"Yes, Orville. Happily. The way this young man looks at his new bride reminds me of you."

Tommy Tulley

Tommy Tulley eats his lunch alone. He walks down the halls alone. He sits on the bus alone.

Who would want to be his friend? Small and bony. Crooked teeth. High-pitched voice. Always wearing a shiny green baseball jacket, stained under the armpits.

Lewis Engler singles him out and mocks him for fun.

"Hey, Mini Man, go somewhere else and eat. Nobody wants to watch you chew your food like that. Oink, Oink."

Everyone at Lewis's table laughs.

Tommy avoids eye contact. He's used to the rejection. He has no friends. He wonders if it will always be like this.

Lewis taunts him again. "If you're coming on the field trip this afternoon, make sure to hang an air freshener around your neck. We don't want you stinking up the bus."

Tommy gets up and shuffles away. Why is Lewis so mean?

Later that afternoon, on the way to the Museum of Natural History, their bus is sideswiped by a gravel truck. The bus driver loses control. The loaded bus flips over a steel guardrail and slides, bouncing, twisting and grinding, to the bottom of a gully, coming to rest backwards and upside down.

The air is choked with dust, debris and the stench of diesel fuel.

Twenty-two passengers have tumbled to the back, blocking the emergency exit. Many in the tightly packed pile of bodies have severe lacerations from scraping along the buckled metal panels.

There is panic in the air.

The bus driver is uninjured and quickly kicks out three side windows. One by one, he pulls the passengers from the screaming, bloody pile and shoves them out a window to safety.

Paramedics arrive within minutes and join the rescue.

Finally, there is only one passenger left inside. Lewis Engler's arm is pinned under the side of the bus through a window that popped out during the rollover.

Tommy, the "Mini Man," sits on the curb, bloodied and dazed. He hears an emergency worker's conversation on a two-way radio: "I can't complete the extrication from inside. There's not enough room for me and my cutting tools. We'll have to raise the rear section."

Suddenly, Tommy jumps to his feet and starts back down the gully to the overturned bus. He enters through a window and slithers all the way to the back, stopping next to Lewis. "I'm small. Maybe they can use me to get the tools under the seat to free you."

Weeping, Lewis grips Tommy with his free hand. "Don't leave me." The bus shifts slightly, and a trickle of dirt sifts down. Lewis screams. "It's like the well!"

Tommy doesn't understand. "The well?"

Lewis gags, then strains to tell the story. "When I was eight, I crawled down an old well because my friends told me there was a box of money buried there.

100

As soon as I got to the bottom, they pulled up the ladder. I screamed for help and clawed at the sides of the well, but they just laughed. My mother came. She pointed her finger at me and said if I was that stupid, I should stay there for a while and learn my lesson. The boys kicked dirt on me, and she didn't stop them. My father finally rescued me when he came home from work."

Now, Tommy understands.

He stays with Lewis until he's rescued.

Lewis spends several weeks in hospital, but fully recovers.

From then on, Lewis invites Tommy, "The Hero," to eat lunch with him and join him and his friends playing cribbage and shuffleboard.

After three lonely, agonizing years at the Bella Vista Seniors' Home, Tommy Tulley, aged seventy-three, finally feels accepted.

The educated hitchhiker

Todd sticks out his thumb as another car merges onto the freeway next to where he's standing.

Two hours by the freeway in the rain drive home the point that he's going nowhere. He's thirty-one, and his Master's degree in Mechanical Engineering has left him with a pile of debt and a bunch of turndowns from employers for being "overqualified."

He's not a seasoned hitchhiker, so he expects brake lights to come on. Finally, they do. A new Mercedes-Benz.

The driver is a man in his sixties, obviously balding, with a perfect comb-over. "I know I'm crazy to pick you up, but what's your story?"

"I'm looking for work, sir."

"Hop in, but don't try any funny stuff. After forty years on the docks, I could still bust a punk like you in half if I had to."

Soaking wet, Todd feels uncomfortable. "Do you have a blanket for me to sit on, sir? I don't want to soak your leather."

"Don't worry about it. I work this Benz hard. Drive a new one every year."

"Wow. You must be well off. How'd you do it?"

"Name's Gordon Parker. I own Parker Shipping International. Fifty million in sales last year. Started out working on the docks and later built my own company from scratch with a grade eight education. Here's my card."

The hitchhiker reaches over to shake his hand. "My name is Todd."

Where you headin'?"

"To be honest, I don't really know. I have a good education, but I'm stuck working night shift for a security company. I have two kids to feed. My wife thinks I've flown out of town for a job interview. I have a few dollars left in my account, but not enough for an airline ticket. I had to get away for a few days to see if I could think of something. I...I think it's hopeless."

"What would you really like to do, son, if you had the money?"

Todd speaks carefully, unsure about risking his ideas with a total stranger. "I've developed a software program for factories to screen new employees. My simulator tests their aptitude for safety and efficiency on specific machines before they're hired."

"That sounds like a winner to me. So, why are you hitchhiking in the rain? Have you tried to sell this to anyone?"

They talk for a hundred miles.

At seven, Gordon stops at a Maverick Jim's Steak House. "I'm buyin' you steak and lobster. You've been starvin' too long." He shakes his head. "Smart guy like you with no money."

They enjoy dinner, dessert and stimulating conversation about business, hard work and sticking with it until you make it.

As he drains his last cup of coffee, Gordon Parker looks Todd straight in the eye. "Son, if you need the bucks to start that computer thing, I'll loan it to you. Wish I had your brains."

Todd turns his head to hide the tears.

"Excuse me, Mr. Parker. I should call my wife and let her know I'm OK."

Gordon waits twenty minutes. Todd doesn't return. He pulls out his credit card and signals their waitress. "Check, please."

Within a minute, she returns and hands him a folded paper. "The young man paid the bill."

"For both of us?"

"Yes, sir. Even left a tip."

Gordon takes out his glasses and reads the note.

Mr. Parker,

I've always had big dreams, but I've been afraid to try. I never knew my father. You inspired me. I promise to call you when I've made it.

Todd

Cash or polish?

The Italian Oxford slips out of his hand, knocking over a bottle of shoe dye.

Marcel grabs his polishing rags and scrambles to soak up the black stain growing on the pure wool carpet.

Mr. Austin leans over his desk with the telephone still in his hand. "You idiot! I've got important stockholders coming this afternoon."

Marcel has just started a new service for corporate executives in the Barris Building. All spring, he's been on the street outside, but he wasn't getting much business. Working people wear Nikes, and businesspeople have no time, so he gathered his courage, went inside and hesitantly offered mobile shoe grooming.

Against all expectations, it worked. So busy they can't stop for a shine, businesspeople willingly kick off their shoes and keep working at their desks in stocking feet while he buffs and brushes. The smell of Kiwi polish fills the office.

Just when he's starting to get ahead, he messes up. Now the president has a pancake-sized, permanent, black stain in front of his desk.

Marcel panics, grabs his polishing box and runs. Down eleven flights of stairs and out the parking lot door.

It's what he always does.

All night, he wanders the waterfront, wrestling with his 'running' problem.

His step-father's voice echoes in his head: "You're a starter but not a finisher. You're just a quitter."

A long string of quittings and leavings. That's what his thirty-seven years have been.

Cheap Chardonnay dulls the pain.

He remembers Mr. Austin's angry blue eyes over his black reading glasses.

Marcel showers in the morning at the men's shelter on 6th Avenue. It's either leave town or go back and face the carpet stain.

At 9:00 a.m., he steps out of the elevator. "I'm here to see Mr. Austin."

"Mr. Austin has clients all day."

"I'll wait."

After three hours, Mr. Austin waves him in impatiently.

"I'll pay for the damage, sir. I have no money, but I'll do whatever it takes to square up with you."

Marcel knows Mr. Austin is busy and probably wishes he would just leave. The company can easily afford to have the carpet replaced.

But Marcel needs this moment. The crucial issue is not Mr. Austin's carpet but Marcel's personal battle.

After a few moments, Mr. Austin unexpectedly gets up from his desk. "Cash or polish, Marcel?"

"I'll polish it off, sir." They both laugh.

"As I see it, you'll need to shine twelve pairs a week for sixteen weeks to clean up your debt. Can I trust you, Marcel?"

Every Monday morning at nine, Marcel is in the reception area as agreed. Each Sunday night, he's had to battle the quitter inside.

On week eleven, Marcel pleads for twelve dollars to buy polish. A secretary has seen him begging on the street. There's a cut above his left eye.

On week sixteen, at 9:00 a.m., the whole office staff assembles. A chocolate cake with sparklers sits on a coffee wagon.

He doesn't show.

At noon, Mr. Austin goes down and questions a panhandler in the street. "Where's Marcel?"

"Got mugged."

Marcel is in a coma from a baseball bat to the back of the neck.

Mr. Austin visits him.

Marcel doesn't know it, but he's actually on staff at Austin Financial. After the twelfth Monday, Mr. Austin included him in the company's generous part-time employee benefit program. He planned to hire him full time as a maintenance man if he stuck it out for sixteen weeks.

Marcel never walks again. The company's disability insurance pays for everything and gives him a lifetime income.

The cruel Munger

Nurse Gail is at the bedside of her family's lifelong enemy.

But Arthur Munger, the man who put Gail's sister in a wheelchair, doesn't recognize her. She was never in his class.

Now, he's old and frail. The woman who's hated him since childhood has just been put in charge of his care at the Derby Hills Rest Home. A good time for revenge?

Munger was hired as a teacher forty-two years ago by Westview Elementary School. His style was unique—forced learning by threats.

He was a small man, with a protruding lower lip, an acne-scarred face and greasy, thinning hair. He ruled his students with a wooden yardstick.

"Roger, you have not completed your assignment on time. This entire class will now face the consequences of your disobedience. No recess today." The yardstick smacked the side of Roger's desk.

Joy "Birdie" Brennan was a timid eighth grade student with a slight speech impediment. Mr. Munger picked on her, ridiculing her attempts to read in front of the class. "You have not prepared yourself properly, as usual. Next Tuesday, you must read an entire chapter out loud. I expect your delivery to be clear and without hesitation."

Birdie suffered severe headaches on Sundays, the day before she had to go back to school.

Tuesday came. She read beautifully from *The Siege of London* by Henry James. On the last page, she mispronounced the word "indissolubly." Munger cracked his yardstick against the blackboard. "You will read TWO chapters next Tuesday. Because of you, this class will be held for thirty minutes after school today."

"I'll never be able to read!" Birdie dropped the book and raced out the front door of Westview School. "I'm just stupid!"

As she jumped the ditch behind the playground, she fell, slicing open her knees. Distracted by the pain, she stumbled across the road. A blue Chevrolet, driven by the local minister, struck her.

That was how Joy "Birdie" Brennan became a quadriplegic. Her entire family blamed Arthur Munger. At the end of the school year, he disappeared.

The local community supported the Brennans. Charitable donations paid for extra therapy. Every year on Birdie's birthday, a financial gift arrived from an anonymous philanthropist, sent by a law firm. Many years, that extra money was all that kept the family from disaster.

After her release from hospital, books became Birdie's greatest pleasure. She still goes to her old school and reads to the children. Her speech impediment is gone.

Now, after all these years, the cruel and abusive Arthur Munger has reappeared as a sickly care home patient.

Nurse Gail, Birdie's younger sister, greets him on his arrival. "Welcome to Derby Hills. I'll be responsible for your health and safety."

Arthur looks relieved. "Thank you, nurse. I'm afraid of medications. I choke easily."

A cold smile crosses her face. "What did you do for a living, sir?"

"I was a teacher for five years, but failed miserably. I was unsure of my abilities and took it out on the students. Many were damaged because of my unnecessary harshness."

The old man continues, "During my last year of teaching, one of my students was badly injured. It was my fault. I never taught again."

"What did you do then?"

"I worked as a janitor until retirement. At least, doing that job, I couldn't hurt anybody. I regret not doing more for the students I hurt. My letters of apology to the Brennans were returned, unopened."

Within six months, Arthur Munger is dead of natural causes.

Birdie's usual financial birthday gift does not arrive this year.

Stanley Crowder's two-ton killing machine

Jordan Ross is on his way to a job he's tired of: department manager at a Webmaster computer store. He's gone as far as he'll ever go with this company.

Coming out of college, he dreamed about a job with a challenging future. Now it's car payments, rent, student loans and an engagement ring to buy before Christmas.

Jordan takes the Madison Street off-ramp and slows for traffic bunching up at the light. Without warning: screeching brakes, body panels crunching and a shower of shattered glass. His rear window disappears, and his Honda SUV is hammered into the back of the delivery truck in front.

Then everything is quiet. He sits motionless for a minute, thankful he's alive.

An elderly gentleman approaches his door. "Are you hurt, son?" His hands are trembling.

Jordan gets out slowly. Glass crunches underfoot. "I think I'm OK, sir. What happened?"

"I hit you fellas from behind. It appears my brakes failed. I'm terribly sorry." He hesitates, then extends his hand. "I'm Stanley Crowder."

Jordan takes the hand. They step back to take a look. Two tons of 1995 Cadillac Fleetwood have driven Jordan's SUV into a delivery truck carrying

111

plate glass. The road is a thick carpet of shattered crystals.

Jordan and Stanley approach the truck. The driver is on his cell phone.

"Are you injured?" asks Mr. Crowder.

The driver explodes. "Why do you still have a driver's license, old man? You're a menace. I think you broke my neck!"

"I'm so sorry," replies Stanley Crowder. "I applied the brake pedal as usual, but my car just kept going."

"That's the trouble with old codgers like you. You've got the reaction time of a slug, yet they let you behind the wheel of a two-ton killing machine. Nobody's safe."

Stanley looks indignant. "I'll have you know that I've been accident-free for over thirty years. This is my first mishap."

The driver begins to roll up his window. "I'm turnin' you in, geezer. I hope they yank your license for good."

Jordan taps on the glass. "Maybe we should move off the road. Rush hour traffic's really backing up."

"I ain't movin' till the cops and paramedics get here. I've got whiplash."

Jordan leads Mr. Crowder back to his white Cadillac.

"That guy's a real jerk," Jordan says. "He doesn't look hurt to me. Do you want me to call someone from your family?"

Emergency vehicles arrive, and everyone gets a ride to the hospital for a check-over. All three drivers are discharged by noon.

Jordan chats with Mr. Crowder on the way out. "Do you use a computer, sir?"

"Why, yes." he replies.

Jordan reaches into his pocket. "Here's my card, Mr. Crowder. Visit my store sometime. I'll show you the latest high tech stuff. And if you have any trouble because of this accident, just call me."

Within days, the delivery driver files a complaint with the Motor Vehicle Branch. Stanley Crowder's license is suspended pending investigation.

The investigation shows that Stanley was driving with the emergency brake engaged. This caused the brakes to heat up, reducing stopping ability by at least fifty per cent.

Stanley is now required to take a driving test.

His vision and reaction times are acceptable, and his license is re-issued. Jordan's statement that Stanley seemed composed and competent after the accident helps. Stanley's insurance pays for the damage. No lawsuits are anticipated.

Early one Tuesday morning, Jordan Ross gets a call at the store. "Jordan, it's Stanley Crowder. Could we go for lunch today? I have coupons for a lunch deal at Wendy's. A free small vanilla Frosty with every Junior cheeseburger meal this week! My oldest son Neil wants to meet you. Since the accident, he's had a number of questions that I couldn't answer."

They meet at 11:40, before the busy lunch line-up begins. Neil is well groomed and wearing a navy blue business suit with black Oxfords. He looks serious, like a man on a mission.

Jordan wonders if there is going to be trouble after all. Stanley's family has not been involved up till now.

Is this a trap?

Stanley goes over his version of the accident story again. Each time it's retold, it seems to be more in Stanley's favor as it relates to his innocence.

A period of uncomfortable silence follows.

Then, Neil stands and pulls a business card from his suit pocket. He offers it to Jordan as if it was a gift from a close friend.

"Mr. Ross, I'm president of Net One Diversified. I have something to ask you. My father said you were kind to him when he had the accident and that you offered to help him with his computer. We're looking for a computer solution specialist, so I made some detailed enquiries. The salary would be twice what you're making now, plus bonuses. Are you interested?"

Eighteen steps

Marlene knows exactly where she's going, although she has not been there for years.

There will be new people in the house now, but maybe they will let her walk on the grass or sit on the rope swing under the birch tree. With the city two hundred miles behind her, and the scent of corn silage in the air, she knows she's made the right decision.

She needs this trip, to stand again on the soil where she was raised.

As she turns off Highway 10 onto Creekside Road, she stares in amazement. Her childhood home and the birch tree swing have been swallowed by a new Valu-Max big box store.

The grand opening celebration is today.

In disbelief, she drives slowly through the congested parking lot.

Free helium balloons. Free pop and hot dogs. Free tire rotation at the auto service center. Rows of newly trained recruits in red vests.

Trying to imagine where her house would have been, she parks her Hybrid Honda beside the garden center and walks slowly towards the celebration.

Methodically, she paces out the number of steps from the ditch on Creekside Road to where her mother's garden would have been. She remembers the warm soil and the colorful seed packets on stakes at the end of each row.

After eighteen steps, she stops in front of a gigantic yellow trash compactor with a harvest of cardboard bales on the pavement beside it.

Marlene Porter, forty-five, is a highly respected chartered accountant with an international firm. She's spent little time with her family during her rise to the top. Now, because of a personal crisis, she needs them.

But her mother and father have been gone for five years. She has a brother somewhere, but they've lost touch.

This trip was her last hope to find personal grounding. Instead, she's lost in a sea of price-cutting hoopla. Her childhood has been erased by a multinational corporation.

The ribbon-cutting ceremony is about to begin.

And then she hears the chant of protesters.

"Valu-Max kills family businesses." The small group pound their signs on the pavement.

Without warning, the chant is overwhelmed by a country band warming up the crowd in preparation for the ribbon cutting.

"Valu-Max sends jobs overseas."

Shoppers ignore the protesters as they rush by to take advantage of forty per cent savings on paper towels piled high on pallets at the front of the store.

Marlene edges closer to the tiny group of dissidents.

"Do you have any more signs?" she asks.

They offer her a chunk of blank cardboard and a black marker.

With great care, she creates her own sign: "Valu-Max destroyed my home." Then, Marlene lofts her sign and joins the shouts of the protesters.

Nobody notices. Nobody cares.

Within the hour, the ribbon has been cut, the band has played the national anthem, and 24-hour shopping is a reality.

Sadly, Marlene deposits her sign in a litter barrel and wanders aimlessly, ending up behind the building. A wire fence separates the giant store from the fields where she played as a child. A metal sign reads: "Sensitive fish and wildlife habitat."

Without hesitation, she climbs over the fence and makes her way down to the shallow creek. That's when she spots the weathered wooden steps among the willows at the water's edge. Her father built them for her because she often cut her feet on the sharp rocks trying to reach the sandy spot in the middle of the creek.

She steadies herself against a moss-covered cedar fence post, slips off her sandals and takes three steps back into her girlhood.

The creek bottom is still the same. Cool sand oozes between her toes.

Tainted family blood

"Tell Great-Gran your name, sweet child, and who you belong to."

Hannah Ballantyne sits stiffly in a mahogany ladder-back chair in her formal dining room, her wispy white hair knotted in a bun.

She's wearing a cranberry cashmere sweater and a white silk blouse closed at the neck with a gold brooch ringed with pearls. The scent of her favorite rose petal perfume surrounds her.

Her delicate left hand is extended to receive the next child waiting in line to wish her well at her eighty-fifth birthday celebration. As per her request, each great-grandchild has brought her a self-made gift.

"Mind your manners now, children," she says firmly. "Girls first. It's common courtesy that young gentlemen will give preference to young ladies." She dabs at her forehead with a lace handkerchief and mutters to herself, "Did good breeding expire at the end of the century?"

Hannah knows each of her fifty-eight family members by name but not always by sight. She suffers from macular degeneration and is now legally blind.

Eight great-granddaughters dutifully present themselves and their gifts, answer questions about their schoolwork, receive a gentle pat on the head and then race down creaky wooden steps into the windowless basement to play hide and seek.

Then, her first great-grandson steps forward.

"I see the shadow of a hat, young man." She motions to him to stand directly in front of her. "It is uncouth for a male to wear his hat indoors. Do your parents not teach you manners?"

She reaches awkwardly for his hat to remove it, and, as she does, her quivering hand comes to rest on short, wiry, Afro hair.

She pulls back with shock and revulsion. "You are undoubtedly a child from 'that man.' I didn't expect you here, but your lack of manners certainly doesn't surprise me, knowing who your father is."

She waves him away. "Now, who is next?"

There is a strained silence.

The rest of the family were surprised to see the mixed-race family attend the birthday party after all the hurtful things Great-Gran said six-and-a-half years ago when Sheila, her fourth granddaughter, married a black businessman in Trinidad.

She told Sheila's mother, "The family blood has been tainted. That man and his offspring will bring all kinds of unsuitable behavior into our family and will disrupt the love and harmony that we all share."

Many of the family had agreed with her.

Sheila steps forward to lead her son away, but he resists. "No! I didn't tell Great-Gran my name yet. And she didn't see my present."

He holds out a crayon drawing of a stick figure wearing over-sized glasses. "I'm Tyson, and I'm six," he lisps. "This is a picture I drew of you looking at me. I drew special 'family' glasses for you so you could see me on your birthday 'cause I was sad that you don't see good. Do you like it?"

Hannah Ballantyne reaches for her cane, grasps the drawing and walks slowly to her bedroom down the hall, closing the door firmly behind her.

The awkward moment hangs oppressively in the room.

Sheila and her husband Grayson stand stone-faced to one side. No one knows what to say or do.

Twenty minutes later, Hannah shuffles back and seats herself in the chair again. Wetness stains the powder on her cheeks. Quietly she says to those in the room, "Bring the boy back."

Tyson is called up from the basement.

She strokes his face gently with frail, trembling hands. "It took me some time to get used to the special glasses you made for me. You are a brilliant inventor, Tyson. I can see you now."

There's a big offer for Moon Pitcher Farm

"You haven't been a good mother. Now you have a chance to make things right."

Odessa Mead leans on her bent-willow porch railing and replies quietly. "I'm not selling this place, Spencer. While I'm on this earth, this farm is my 'forever place.' From my front porch I watch the crescent moon settle on top of Slot Canyon and become a pitcher, pouring crystal water onto the rainbow rock below."

Spencer replies, "Everyone says you're a crazy old flower child who never got past her hippie days. It's not normal to live out here alone, walking barefoot, with goats following you around."

Odessa Mead is a tall woman with a leathery complexion and a waist-length, gray French braid. She's flexible and graceful and glides across the ground as if not wanting to disturb the soil underfoot.

She wipes her eyes with a corner of her green flannel shirt. "It makes me sad to hear you talk this way. If only you could have been happy here too, then my life would be complete. How many times have I written and begged you to visit me? I had goat cheese, stone-ground bread and strawberries from my garden ready for you, but you never came back."

All her life she has felt unwanted. Born to older parents, she was considered their "burden" until she left the farm at eighteen to marry a young man from the city.

At the time, her teenaged husband thought it might be cool to live "in nature," and they settled here beside Moon Pitcher Falls. The marriage didn't last. He moved back to the city, leaving her to raise her son alone.

As soon as he was old enough, Spencer also ran off to the city.

Odessa still lives by candlelight and draws her water from the pool at the base of the falls.

She's even too shy to talk to her customers who buy honey from the "honor system" stand at the road.

Her son is here today because he has been contacted by a large resort company that wants to purchase Moon Pitcher Farm and develop it as a conference center.

When a representative came by a week ago to give her a proposal, his mother hid in the goat shelter.

Spencer glares at her. "Mother, don't you realize how hard it was for me, growing up here with no electricity and no friends? Don't you know how hard it was to make a life for myself starting out with no money and no education?"

In the background is the drowsy drone of bees making honey.

"Listen, Mother. Westrock Resorts will pay big money for this property. Here's your chance to make things up to me."

Odessa looks down. "But I don't want the money. I wish you could feel this land in your soul like I do."

"This is not my home. It never was."

She looks at him with fearful, darting, dark brown eyes. "Where will I live when I'm old?"

"You'll have more than enough money to decide. Come back with me and sign the offer. It will be best for both of us."

"No, son, this is my home. Money can't buy the joy I feel here."

Spencer steps off the deck and calls over his shoulder, "You don't care about what's best for me, and you don't trust me."

Three weeks later, he receives an unexpected note: "I'm ready to sign it over."

At the lawyer's table, Odessa pulls out a tattered piece of lined paper. "Here are my instructions."

The paper reads: "It is my belief that my son, Spencer Mead, has his mother's best interests at heart and will do what is right. I hereby gift sole legal title of Moon Pitcher Farm to him."

Goodbye, Chatterbox

Tonya Carter hasn't seen her dad for twenty years.

He last hugged her when she was seven. She remembers his Old Spice aftershave and the way his whiskers tickled her face. His last words were, "Goodbye, Chatterbox. Make room for another bear."

His job with an industrial supply company took him away from home for long periods of time. He promised her a new stuffed animal every trip, and the shelf above her bed was full of plush, wild creatures. Her favorite was a fluffy cinnamon bear named "Cubby."

After this trip, he didn't come home when expected. Her mother had angry words on the phone and cried all weekend.

Tonya never saw him again.

Many Friday nights, she waited up late for the sound of his car in the driveway, but he never came back. Cubby and his animal friends on the shelf were all very sad.

"Daddy's working very hard," her mother explained. After that, she changed the subject whenever Tonya asked about him.

Tonya was in her teens before she found out about the support payments that came every month in envelopes with slanted blue writing.

During her senior year in college, she tried desperately to find her dad. Her mother was ill and not expected to live. Unfortunately, that year, Tonya buried her mother without finding him.

The support payments stopped the month she graduated. That was five years ago.

At 2:30 a.m. one Tuesday night, she hears his voice again on the phone. "Tonya, this is your dad." His speech is slurred and raspy. "I need to talk to you."

Horrified, she hangs up.

By the next day, she's desperately hoping he'll call back, but he doesn't.

She checks her call display and dials the number. It's a payphone.

The next evening, Tonya drives her yellow Beetle slowly past a number of taverns looking for him. A drunk on the sidewalk stumbles towards her car. "Hey, baby, take me home. I'll make you happy." She hits the gas and hurries back to her apartment.

She tells herself to forget him. "No good father abandons his own daughter."

After two sleepless nights, she begins another serious search. She finally finds him at a men's shelter downtown.

They meet in the coffee shop of the Mercury Hotel.

Lyle pours an avalanche of sugar into his green-striped mug and tries to focus his bloodshot eyes on her. "How you been, sweetheart?"

Twenty years of her bottled-up emotions burst forth. "How've I been!?"

He swallows. "The doc at the clinic says I probably only have a couple a months left. Cirrhosis. I've been a drunk most of my whole life. I managed to hold it together till about five years ago. Then..."

She can't believe it. "All my life, you've never been there for me. All those years growing up, I wanted a father, but you weren't there. When Mom died, I

125

needed you, but you weren't there. Now, when you're old and sick and you need me, you show up."

A bleach-blonde waitress approaches their table. "You know this creep?"

"He's my father."

Tonya sobs, realizing what she's just said. She takes a breath and looks at him. "If you're willing to go into rehab, there's an extra bedroom in my apartment. I guess you can stay there."

He shakes his head. "I don't deserve anything from you."

Then he pulls a stained and tattered envelope from the inside pocket of his gray wool coat. "I want you to have this."

It's a letter from a law firm. The purpose of the letter is to inform him of a large number of valuable stocks issued in his name by the industrial supply company he'd worked for all his life until he was fired five years ago.

He says, "I've always loved you, Chatterbox. Do you still have Cubby?"

Heartbroken over Harold

"Mr. Hansen, we want to adopt Harold. We want him to be our son."

"That's impossible," states the adoption lawyer. Harold's become a ward of the state. Besides, his mother is still alive. Just because she's terminally ill doesn't mean folks like you can apply to take her son away. She has legal rights, you know. Why don't you just forget about this?"

Brett's face is flushed with frustration. "You make it sound like we're swooping in to steal a dying widow's son. Harold lives next door to us. We've looked after him many times while Wilma's been ill. He's lonely, withdrawn and afraid at the interim care home. His mother suggested this."

Brett and Cara-Mae Nelson are in their late thirties. Both work. He's a firefighter. She's a dental hygienist.

They can't have children. Cara-Mae's doctor has suggested adoption.

Their neighbor, Wilma Foster, was widowed when her son, Harold, was five. She's done a remarkable job as a single mother.

Harold has developmental challenges—Down syndrome. He's loving and affectionate. Always tells you exactly what he's thinking. He's slightly overweight (chubby in the middle), loves peanut butter on toast and wears denim overalls with metal buttons. His Uncle Ray gave him a blue New York

Yankees baseball cap that he keeps protected in a plastic bag inside a shoebox. He wears it on his birthday.

He loves robins and watches them for hours. He wishes he could fly and land on telephone wires. His personal philosophy about the birds in his backyard is: "Don't...don't...like black...black...crows. Cawing, nasty. Robins smart. Ears listen for...for...noisy worms. Pretty red stomach. Friendly."

Wilma has accepted that she's dying. She can't possibly care for Harold anymore because of her heavy medication. Her social worker arranged for a family to take him during her illness, and she reluctantly agreed. She had no choice.

Wilma cries herself to sleep worrying about her son. Do these people know he likes his toast cut into triangles to dip into soft poached eggs? What about spreading the last piece with peanut butter and drawing a happy face in it? That's the only way he'll eat all of his breakfast.

Neighbors Brett and Cara-Mae have been stopping by every day to check on her. They feed Ruckles the poodle and cut her lawn on Saturdays.

"Can you bring Harold back for a visit?" Wilma pleads. "I feel like I've abandoned him."

They check with the social worker. She feels it might upset him even more to come back for such a short time. He doesn't handle change very well.

Everyone is heartbroken over Harold.

Brett, Cara-Mae and Wilma have spent countless hours talking about his future. "I can't bear to see him living with strangers," Wilma sobs. "He'll never be like a son to them. Would you folks adopt him?"

Back in the office of Hansen, Drummond and Essex, the lawyer is perplexed. "I've never heard of anyone wanting to adopt a forty-eight-year-old man with Down syndrome. Why would you bother? His maximum life expectancy is probably around sixty. You will be caring for an aging man. Why don't you folks do the normal thing and adopt a child? Let our social system look after Harold. They have programs for men like him."

Brett and Cara-Mae are determined. They consider their options and apply to be granted "power of attorney for personal care" for Harold. He will live with them as part of their family.

Wilma, seventy-two, passes away soon after. Finally, she can let go.

There's a "For Sale" sign on Cara-Mae's silver BMW. She's not working anymore. This arrangement didn't come with a monthly check from the government. She's at home with Harold and Ruckles, his squirrel-chasing poodle.

There are triangles of toast for dipping, one with peanut butter and a happy face. There is a blue Yankees baseball cap on their mantle. Brett and Cara-Mae have a son.

Open the chute

"Ladies and gentleman, next up in chute number three is H-Bomb. This rank, black bull has only ever been rode once, and that was by Cody Rockwell, the tough, young cowboy they call 'Guts'."

The rodeo announcer's voice softens. "Cody's not with us tonight. He's in a different kinda rodeo right now, takin' on the toughest ride of his life, bone cancer."

Cody never thought about dying in the arena. Whatever fear he had in the chute he channeled into the bull.

But a pretty, bald-headed girl named Lacey has just given him the scare of his life in the chemo unit at Northridge Hospital.

They've already been through rounds of chemo and radiation together. At first, he wouldn't talk. Always looking away and pulling down that black cowboy hat. But gradually she got through to him. They're on the same road. Each has six months to two years to live.

From the time she was a little girl, Lacey's green eyes would dance when she got an idea, and then there was no stopping her. Top marks in school. First violin in the college orchestra. Captain of the women's volleyball team. What she wants badly, she usually gets.

It's Tuesday morning. They've finished their treatment and are walking slowly down the long, white hallway. Lacey stops, presses him gently against the wall and tips back his old black hat. Her green eyes dance.

"I need you, Cody. Neither one of us might have another chance. Marry me, cowboy."

Cody pulls away and runs, but the chemo has made him unstable. He ends up sprawled in front of the nurses' station like a busted-up bull rider in the dirt.

Two nurses help him to his feet. He glances at Lacey, then looks away. "I just can't."

"Why not?" Lacey bites back her tears. "Aren't I pretty enough for you? Would you marry me if I had my hair?"

Cody is shocked. "It's not that. You're the prettiest, smartest woman I ever met. But why would you want to marry a dyin' cowboy?"

Finally, she gets it. "Cody Rockwell, you're chicken! Big tough guy in the chute, taking chances every time you ride, but not enough guts to love me as I am?"

Cody shuffles away. The next morning, he reschedules his treatments to be on different days.

Two weeks later, Cody's sitting alone in the chemo unit watching bull riding on TV as H-Bomb throws another rider.

Cody asks the nurse for a phone. He dials and quietly gets the words out: "Lacey, you're right. I'm afraid I ain't got what it takes to make a good husband. But if you're sure you want to take a chance on this cowboy, open the chute. I'm ready."

Three months after the wedding, something unusual shows up in Lacey's tests. She phones him from the lab. "Cody, we're going to be a real family."

Cody swings his legs over the side of his hospital bed and throws his old black cowboy hat high enough to hit the ceiling.

One year later, at the national championships, the rodeo announcer asks the crowd for their attention. "We've lost two of professional rodeo's best this week. Cody 'Guts' Rockwell didn't make the whistle yesterday in his final battle with cancer. And the big, black bull named H-Bomb that nobody but Cody ever rode was killed when the stock trailer bringing him here flipped on Highway 11. Let's give these two legends a minute of silence, folks."

Mrs. Lacey Rockwell fully recovers and becomes a pink ribbon advocate for cancer survivors.

Cody Jr. insists on wearing a black cowboy hat just like the bull rider in the painting above the fireplace.

Quarter-fold

A bearded man in a dirty red ski jacket sits on a rock reading a tightly folded newspaper. A yellow woman's bike with a laundry basket wired to the handlebars lies beside him.

When Lance McArthur's silver BMW stops at the light nearby, the bearded man jumps up and taps on his window.

Lance hesitates, then slides the tinted window down.

"Can you spare a few bucks for breakfast? I wanna get me some of them all-you-can-eat buttermilk pancakes at IHOP."

Lance is skeptical. "Breakfast? Yeah, right..."

"I promise. If you don't believe me, come and eat with me."

"Maybe some other time." Lance doesn't mean it. But he pulls out his wallet and hands over a ten-dollar bill.

He expects the homeless man will probably just buy alcohol or cigarettes or drugs. His forty-four years have taught him that people don't keep their promises. That fact fuels most of his law practice, but for some reason he has decided to give this man a chance.

The homeless man reaches his tobacco-stained hand through the window of the BMW and says, "God bless you, sir. My name is Peter."

Lance takes the man's hand for a moment. It's thick and warm and smells of dirt and stale smoke.

The light changes, and Lance moves on. But at the next intersection, he has to pull into the parking lot of a Chevron station. He's become emotional, unable to drive safely.

That thick, warm hand reminds him of his father's hand years ago. Once a week, his father would press a bill into his smaller hand. "Remember where you got this, boy."

But it was the newspaper that really did it, the way the man folded it in quarters. Lance's father read the paper every morning on his covered deck overlooking the Pacific, the financial pages folded in quarters against the ocean breezes.

Lance's father gave him everything. Every year, he paid for Lance to play little league, but he never kept his promise to watch his son play third base. His father paid his way through law school, but the year Lance graduated, his father was in Barbados meeting a new client and missed the ceremony.

Lance hasn't spoken to him for over a year.

Now, a homeless man named Peter sitting on a rock reading a folded newspaper has brought the memories flooding back.

"Is it time to call Dad?" he wonders.

Lance picks up his cell phone and then puts it down.

"What would I even say? Would I tell him I just became a partner in the biggest law firm in the city? Would that even matter to him?"

Ten minutes go by, and finally Lance pulls back into the rush hour traffic. Now late for his first appointment, he inches forward impatiently.

For a full minute, he is stopped in front of IHOP. The "All You Can Eat Pancakes" sign over the entrance makes him hungry. He was up at six this morning preparing for a case and missed breakfast.

Lance looks to his right and, startled, spots the yellow woman's bike with the laundry basket leaning against the wall of the restaurant.

As he parks his BMW in the IHOP parking lot, he picks up his cell phone again. The promise kept by a homeless man has given him hope to try one more time.

A recorded message comes on. "This is the Peter McArthur residence. If this is a business call, contact McArthur Securities. If it's personal, leave your number, and we'll contact you when convenient."

"Dad, it's Lance. I'm just meeting someone important for breakfast, but we need to talk today. Call me."

It matters a lot
what you do with the ashes

"My mother won't be dumped in some swampy pond in the middle of the wilderness just because that's where you want your ashes scattered."

In the family lounge at Mercer Memorial Gardens, Vivian Lowery cradles the plastic urn containing her mother's remains. She looks anxiously towards the funeral director seated across from her and her older brother Mitch.

"Well, you can be sure I won't allow my mother to be spread out over fifty strangers in some memorial garden," says Mitch "There's still enough room on this earth to put her somewhere peaceful. God knows, she had a difficult enough life."

Vivian sets her jaw. "I have something to say about this, Mitch. You always tell me what to do, but not this time. This is too important."

"You'll take five years to decide and then probably lose her somewhere in that mess you live in," replies Mitch coldly.

The funeral director leans towards them. He speaks slowly, almost reverently. "We all have a special place we dream of for our loved ones. It's not unusual for family members to have different thoughts on this matter." Then he stands erect. "May I suggest that each of you take a portion of your mother's remains? Then you will have the freedom to say goodbye at your own special place."

"We can do that?" asks Vivian.

"Yes," replies the funeral director. "Some families request multiple urns to do what is known as a 'multiple scattering' of their loved one's ashes."

"Then, divide her up exactly fifty-fifty," says Mitch. "I loved her just as much as my sister did."

Within the hour, two urns are ready at the front office. Mitch has chosen natural biodegradable clay, while Vivian decided on a durable plastic container covered in red silk with a gold clasp at the top.

On the weekend, Mitch takes the clay urn to a crystal blue lake at the base of a rocky mountain ridge and scatters the remains slowly, from his red canoe, at sunset.

Vivian sets the silk-covered urn on top of her dresser and begins to plan.

Her mother's life was hard and messy. Why did she get a mother who scrambled every day to save herself from her own self-created chaos?

The first month, she decides she will rake the ashes into the soft soil beside the white rail fence on the farm where her mother was raised. From then on, every month, she has a different idea—until, ten months later, her mother's remains are under a pile of sweaters and shopping bags on her dresser. That's where they are when her apartment is robbed.

The thief grabs her laptop computer, her green canvas purse and the silk-covered urn, because it looks like a jewelry box.

By coincidence, Mitch calls her that day. "Have you done it yet?"

"No," Vivian sobs. "Some thief just stole her."

"You never do things right. He's probably dropped her in the nearest dumpster."

"I couldn't do it yet, Mitch. I wasn't ready."

"Well, now, because of your stupidity, you'll never have the chance."

In spite of his harsh words, Mitch rushes over and pokes through all the dumpsters in her neighborhood. He doesn't find his mother.

Six days later, a poorly wrapped brown paper package appears on the balcony of Vivian's apartment. The shaky handwriting on the note inside is in black felt marker. It reads, "I grabbed your stuff cause I need bucks more than you. Once I knew what this was, I chucked it in a dumpster. But it spooked me out when I saw her picture on your laptop. Wish I knew where they put my ma. Nobody will tell me."

A rattle of chains

Ella Flynn's graveside funeral is a quiet, dignified affair, befitting the woman herself.

At her request, a choir from Hellmer Elementary School starts the funeral.

The sun shines through a shimmering maple tree, warming the fresh soil next to her grave.

White-haired Reverend Robson addresses the mourners. "Ella's life was truly a gift offered up for others. That is clearly evidenced by the number and quality of people gathered here today to honor her memory."

At that moment, a dark green government van edges its way past the parked vehicles. The minister pauses, waiting for the intruding vehicle to pass by.

Instead, it double-parks next to the hearse, emergency flashers blinking. Two armed guards assist a prisoner out of the van. He's mid-twenties, heavily tattooed and handcuffed.

The funeral guests draw back in horror as the man approaches the graveside. They turn their heads, afraid, not wanting to make eye contact with the criminal.

Uncomfortably, the minister continues with his remarks. "Although she never married, few women have impacted the lives of young children as Ella has."

Unexpectedly, the prisoner begins to weep, his chest heaving with emotion. Without warning, he curses loudly and falls to his knees at the edge of the grave.

He raises his cuffed hands above his head and wails, "Why'd she hafta die so quick? I promised her."

The crowd pulls away even further, and parents cover their children's ears. The guards jerk him to his feet and drag him back, ten feet away from everyone else.

The crowd is aghast. Who is this man who has ruined Ella's funeral?

Reverend Robson clears his throat loudly to regain control of the service and motions for the mourners to come forward again. He reads a well-known Bible verse: "But the greatest of these is love." Motioning toward Ella's photo on top of the rose-strewn casket, he states, "Ella's life was an excellent example of unconditional love."

He continues. "In the last few days, the funeral home has received numerous tributes describing the impact Ella had on people's lives." He shuffles through a number of printed emails. Pulling one out he says, "This is perhaps the most memorable. I'm sure it expresses what many of us have experienced."

He begins to read:

Miss Flynn was my crossing guard for three years when I went to Hellmer Elementary. Seeing her smile every morning made me happy. My mother was hardly ever home, but Miss Flynn always had a brown lunch bag for me when I came to school with nothing to eat. Even after I grew up, she was the only one who ever remembered my birthday. I got her last card two weeks ago. She never gave up on me and always told me I could make something of my life. I didn't

believe it for a long time, but today I do. Miss
Flynn is the only woman who ever cared about
me my whole life.

The mourners are touched. Many are wiping away tears. The letter has expressed so well what all of them feel.

Reverend Robson continues. "The letter is from Leon Worley. Is Mr. Worley here?"

There is an awkward silence. The name is not familiar. People look at each other, wondering who he is.

There is a rattle of chains as the prisoner raises his hands. "I'm Leon. I told a guard what to say and he sent it for me. I'm here to tell ya, I love this woman. I promised her I was gonna straighten out my life, and I'm gonna keep that promise."

Salmon Valley Songsters

Like a spider awaiting her prey, Angie Griffin sits in her spotless International tow truck.

She's parked behind a loading dock in the medical center parking lot. Within the hour, an older gentleman walks out to witness the slim brunette in white coveralls winching his white Toyota Camry onto her flat-deck truck.

"Excuse me, Miss. There must be some mistake. I come here once a week for my blood pressure check."

"New rules, mister. It's pay parking now. You blind?"

"No, just very surprised. Now slide my car back down or I'm calling the police."

Angie secures a safety chain. "Go ahead. They'll tell you to read City Ordinance 314, like it says on the sign."

"But I didn't see the sign."

"That's what they all say."

After considerable protest, he rides with her to the compound, pays the $131.75 and redeems his Toyota. As he puts his wallet away, he grumbles, "You need to get a heart, lady."

Angie's eyes flash. "Why should I give you a break? No one ever gave me one."

Her husband took off three years ago and left her with nothing but this tow truck and a pile of debt. She was positive she could make money with the truck, and she's proving it now. Another year, and the debt will be gone.

She's making her way back to the medical center when the dispatcher calls. "Got a white, twelve-passenger Dodge van, Highway 12 at the Marsden overpass. The horn's stuck."

Within ten minutes, she spots the older van with two white-haired gentlemen looking cautiously under the hood.

She parks, flips on her flashers and walks up to the taller of the two. Over the sound of the horn, she yells, "How you gonna pay? Credit card or cash?"

Then she hears the music. Seven others inside the van are singing "Sentimental Journey" at the top of their lungs.

Angie yanks out a fuse. The horn quits.

"Salmon Valley Songsters" is written across the side of the van. Pictures of black kids are taped to the windows.

Angie sizes up the five men and four women. All are in their seventies or eighties. All are wearing white, heart-shaped buttons with the words "Maison d'Espoir" written in red.

The tall one holds out his hand. "I'm Bert, the piano player."

"You're actually musicians?"

"You bet. We're singers for hope. Five years ago, Henry and Esther took a trip to Haiti. They met a widow named Marie-Maude Paul, who feeds orphaned children with AIDS in an old warehouse she calls 'Maison d'Espoir.' It means 'House of Hope'."

"Cash or credit card?" Angie repeats.

Bert continues. "When they got back, Henry and Esther inspired the rest of us. Since then, we've been

143

putting on concerts to raise money for food and medicine. We sing the good old songs."

Bert smiles and offers Angie a white, heart-shaped button along with the payment and a little extra for herself. "Thanks for coming so quickly. The horn blowing was very disturbing to those of us who can't turn our hearing aids down."

As Angie drives away, she hears them start an old favorite. Nine joyful voices singing "Cruising Down the River on a Sunday Afternoon."

One year later, she's still hauling away cars at the medical center. A woman in a designer outfit chews her out. "You're preying on the sick!"

Angie keeps her hand firmly on the winch. She smiles. "The way I figure it, you've got a Volvo and a medical plan. Most people in the world don't get breaks like that."

As she writes out the charges, she points to a white, heart-shaped button on her coveralls. "Look lady, fifteen per cent of your tow bill goes straight to feed orphaned kids in Haiti. Got any more to say?"

With his Corvette idling

"Don't expect too much, Keith. Our house is nothing like yours. Mom's been sick a lot lately, and Dad's been short of work this year."

Joanne Ritter, twenty-one, is bringing her fiancé home to meet her family for the first time. She's nervous.

She moved to the city six months ago and got a job at Maclure Insurance. The second day, she met the man of her dreams, the owner's son. Keith Maclure is over six feet tall with sandy blond hair and powder blue eyes. He golfs a lot but works most afternoons for a few hours as his duty to the family business.

As he pulls his white Corvette into the driveway of Joanne's parents' home, Keith's eyes widen with surprise. "You grew up here? In all this junk?"

Two rusty Buicks sit on the overgrown lawn with faded "For Sale" signs taped to the windshields.

Two topless washing machines and a dented dryer greet them at the bottom of the front steps.

Dozens of her family members are waiting for the couple.

Her father has a sweating can of Coors in his hand. "Happy to hear Joanne's marryin' the boss's son. Maybe she can send home a few bucks like we planned when we sent her to the city."

Awkwardly, Keith reaches out his hand. "Nice to meet you, Mr. Ritter. You've raised an amazing daughter."

Joanne's older brother Jack motions Keith into the back hall. He puts his arm around Keith's neck and gives him a brotherly warning: "Don't you mess with our little sister now, big city boy. She's the prettiest gal this town's ever seen. You treat her right, or you'll deal with all us Ritter boys."

Joanne's mother comes over and offers Keith a cold meat and mayonnaise sandwich. She steers him into the kitchen where the ladies are gathered around Joanne, gasping at the size of the diamond.

Joanne looks up at her fiancé and knows immediately that something is terribly wrong. He motions for her to join him in the hall. "I'm not comfortable here, Joanne." They leave the party early.

On the way back to the city, Keith turns up the music and doesn't speak.

Halfway home, he stops beside the highway. With his Corvette idling, he leans over and takes her hand. "I'm sorry, Joanne, but I know now that I can't marry you. We're from different worlds. I don't want to raise my children around those people. I've always imagined only the best for my kids."

She cries for weeks, blaming her parents for her loss, but she's determined to stay in the city.

*****

Twenty-five years later, Joanne's nineteen-year-old daughter Megan brings home a blond, blue-eyed guy named Tyler she met at university. In the kitchen, she whispers, "Mom, I think he's the one."

He sits nervously on the sofa and glances around her neat, middle-class living room. "You have a wonderful home," he says. "Megan talks about it all the time. She was so lucky to grow up here with parents

146

who loved her and sacrificed to send her to university."

Joanne, recently widowed, nods.

Tyler continues. "I wasn't so lucky. When I was three, my parents divorced. My Dad had married the mayor's daughter, but she made his life miserable. After their divorce, he fought to keep custody of me. He did his best to raise me, but it was hard growing up without a mother. Dad says he married the wrong woman. He was once engaged to a secretary at his dad's company, Maclure Insurance, but he broke off the engagement. He always regretted it. Said it was the biggest mistake of his life."

She stole
The Grapes of Wrath

"Wanda, two police officers are leading your mother through the mall. They just came out of Buchanan's bookstore."

"Is she OK? Did she fall?"

"I don't know. She's pulling her little oxygen cart and seems to be dragging her feet. You better get down here."

Wanda Patton thanks her cosmetician for calling and runs to her car in the parking lot of the accounting firm where she works.

She thinks, "Why didn't they call an ambulance? Maybe she's having a heart attack."

Wanda rushes into the bookstore. There's a line-up at the cash register. She interrupts a clerk taking a customer's payment. "What happened to my mother, the older lady with the oxygen cart?"

The clerk motions for Wanda to wait. She lowers her voice. "I'll be with you in a moment. Your mother had a little mishap."

"What kind of mishap?" Wanda raises her voice.

The clerk's eyes begin to smolder. "Can't you see I'm helping a customer?"

Wanda won't move. "What happened to my mother? Where is she?"

The clerk throws up her hands. "Well, if you want everyone to know, your mother was arrested for shoplifting. She stole *The Grapes of Wrath*, hardcover, right off the front table."

"Stole? She's a seventy-five-year-old great-grandmother. Why would she steal a book?"

"She stole it all right. Browsed around the store with it in her hand for half an hour, then stashed it in the tank bag of her little cart. Security caught everything on video, and she was detained the second she stepped into the mall."

"You called the police on an old lady with an oxygen tank?"

"It's our policy, ma'am. No exceptions. We prosecute all shoplifters to the full extent of the law."

Wanda is embarrassed. For some time, she's been afraid her mother's been losing it. Ruth hasn't been the same since her husband Herb died two years ago.

At the police station, Wanda rushes up to the enquiry desk. "Are you holding a Mrs. McCormick here?"

"Yes. Are you a relative?"

"I'm her daughter. I must see her immediately."

Ruth is sitting on a gray, steel chair with her chin sagging against her ivory wool sweater.

Wanda kneels in front of her. "Mother, did you take the book?"

Ruth nods.

"Why?"

"Because it's your father's favorite book, dear. I wanted a new hardcover for him, and there never seems to be enough money from our pension checks."

Wanda turns to the police officer. "My mother is a little confused these days. She didn't know what she was doing. Can I just pay for the book? I'm sure this won't happen again."

The officer frowns. "I'm afraid not. The store insisted on laying charges. We can't just let her go."

Unexpectedly, Ruth joins their conversation. "Why not? You policemen did it when Wanda stole that fold-up stroller for baby Joel."

"What?" Wanda is reeling. For thirty years, she's kept quiet about her desperate act as a very young mother with a new baby and no extra money. She still shudders when she remembers being arrested and taken to the police station. She couldn't believe it when, out of the blue, someone paid the store and the officer said she could go without being charged.

Wanda stares open-mouthed at her mother. "You knew?"

Ruth takes her daughter's hand and speaks clearly. "A friend of mine who worked in the mall saw the police take you, dear. She paid for the stroller, and I paid her back over the next three months out of my egg money."

Wanda gasps. "My greatest fear all these years was that you'd find out. Why didn't you say something?"

"You were a wonderful mother, Wanda. I knew it wouldn't happen again."

A.J. doesn't know
where to stand

Martha Jennings whispers weakly to her son, "Cecil, stop fussing over me and help that young man with his mother. He doesn't know what to do. He doesn't even know where to stand when the nurses are with her."

Cecil glances at the muscular young man with the jagged scar on his cheek pacing beside the woman in the next bed.

"I can't educate everyone on how to attend to their sick relatives," replies Cecil. "My main concern right now is you. I can't care about him."

Martha's eyes flash. "I raised you to care!"

Then her voice softens. "Cecil, I know my time is short and I'm going home. That boy's mother is so young. Help him, Cecil—for my sake."

Cecil bends down and speaks softly to his thin, pale, ninety-two-year-old mother. "I don't want to get involved. That's the woman who was in the paper, the one beaten by the drug addict. Those people aren't like us in the least. For our own safety, I think we should just mind our own business."

The newspaper reports said the woman's boyfriend demanded money for drugs. When she didn't have enough, he crushed her skull with a workout weight and left her bleeding on the floor, grabbing her TV as he left.

The paper also said the woman's son, A.J. Taggert, was eighteen and didn't live at home. He's the young man with the scar and the black wool skull cap in the room with them now.

A.J. continues to pace back and forth in front of his mother's bed, constantly texting on his cell phone.

As a nurse approaches, he asks in an uncertain voice, "Is she gonna make it? Why's she sometimes jerkin' like that?"

The nurse replies crisply, "Your mother is in critical condition. Please wait outside the room while I administer her medication."

A.J. pounds the steel railing of his mother's bed with his fist and moves out into the hall. As he approaches the ICU waiting room, he kicks the steel doorframe.

Cecil's mother pleads with her son to join A.J. in the waiting room. "All your life, you've had a family loving you, taking care of you and giving you guidance. I'm sure this boy's had none of that."

They sit across from each other in silence, two men with dying mothers: an eighteen-year-old street kid and a seventy-year-old retired accountant. One slouched in his chair wearing a black skull cap, and the other sitting upright in a brown tweed jacket.

After a lengthy silence, Cecil says, "That's my mother in there beside your mother."

A.J. shrugs.

"My mother is dying," Cecil continues. "When she passes, I'm really going to miss her, but it's been wonderful to have had someone who cared about me my whole life."

A.J. looks up and says, "If my Mom dies, I don't even know what to tell them to do with her body. Do you know?" Then, without waiting for the answer, he stands and starts dialing his phone. "Wanna pizza? I'm starvin' here."

Later that night, A.J.'s mother's beaten body gives up the struggle to breathe. A.J. wails out his anguish against the bed rail, promising revenge. Cecil puts an arm over the boy's heaving shoulders.

From that moment, Cecil takes charge and guides A.J. through the funeral arrangements.

During the service, the air in the chapel is thick with despair, anger and revenge. Tattoos and body piercings are everywhere. Funeral staff are nervous.

A.J. takes the microphone. "I don't want no trouble. Mom's seen enough." He points to Cecil in the front row. "You all gotta know. If it wasn't for this dude and his mother, I'da hunted that animal down and done him myself."

Poster boy

"Mom, I'm at the pool. I need to go away for a while. There's some guys following me."

Then the phone goes dead. That's the last Gina Gardner hears from her sixteen-year-old son.

The police get a tip that he was taken by two men in a white truck. They think he's dead.

Nine months later, Gina still rolls her red suitcase around the city putting up yellow "Missing" posters. The "poster lady" has been in the news.

Hundreds of posters are still up. A photo of a teenaged boy with long, wavy hair and glasses. The police phone number and the date he went missing. A description of Matthew James Gardner: five-foot-eleven, one hundred and sixty pounds, blue eyes, freckles, braces, a small scar on his left baby finger. "$5,000 REWARD" in heavy black marker.

It's 7:00 a.m., and Harold Hamilton has just put up five yard sale signs on poles in his subdivision. He and his wife are selling out and moving south. As he opens his garage door, he sees a short, thirty-something woman with swollen, stubby fingers staple a yellow "Missing" poster over his new sign on the pole beside the driveway.

He approaches her. "I'm sorry, ma'am, but that sign is for our sale today. Please move yours."

She looks at him with grieving eyes. "You care more about selling old furniture than helping a mother find her son?"

Harold's voice changes. "You're the poster lady, aren't you? I understand that you are upset about your son being missing, but you can't abuse public space like this. People are searching for our yard sale."

Gina stands her ground. "If you take it down, I'll just put another one up."

"Lady, you're crazy. You've got posters up all over town. One more isn't going to make a difference."

Her shoulders sag, and her eyes plead. "If you help me find my son, I'll pay you five thousand dollars."

Harold shakes his head as he walks back to his garage. He drags a wooden stepladder to the curb and tapes on a hastily made cardboard sign above Gina's. He doesn't believe Gina has enough money to pay a reward. She's just a bent-over lump of sadness pulling a red suitcase around town.

With a final, hopeless stare at Harold, Gina turns and walks off down the street. She mutters sadly, "Nobody helps anybody anymore. All people care about is money."

Meanwhile, people are arriving for the yard sale.

At 10:00 a.m., a muddy, white truck pulls into the driveway. Two men who look like farmers head for the used tools. "How long is the big tape measure?" asks the younger one.

"Fifty feet," replies Harold.

While stretching it out, the prospective buyer ends up next to the power pole. He notices the poster, looks at it carefully and then calls to the other man. "Dad, isn't this the freaked-out kid we gave a ride to last summer? Isn't he still working for that chicken farmer in Willow Butte?"

Harold convinces the men to wait in his driveway.

Leaving his wife to work the yard sale, he searches frantically and finally finds the poster lady sitting on a green, metal bench at the back entrance to the swimming pool.

"Mrs. Gardner, I know where Matthew is. Two men in a white truck are waiting in my driveway. Hurry. I'll take you."

She reaches into her red suitcase and pulls out a baking soda can. "Who do I owe the five thousand to?" she asks tearfully. "Them or you?"

"I don't know about them, but I don't want your money, Mrs. Gardner," says Harold quietly. "I was wrong about the poster. One more did make the difference."

In the family way

"I will not forgive!"

She folds the letter for the fourth time and buries it under the books on her reading table. The letter is written with a fountain pen.

Dear Marilyn:

I have always meant to apologize for your expulsion from medical school. I chose not to believe your explanation, only because it was expedient for me."

My decision, as dean, was improper. I thought of you many times over the years, as medical school graduates took the Hippocratic Oath and began their careers. You were born to be a physician. My actions robbed you of the opportunity to complete your calling.

I am now eighty-two years of age and in poor health. It is my desire to put my affairs in order before I pass from this life. Your forgiveness is requested.

With deep sincerity,
Dean Ralston Horvath

Marilyn Vanderberg was the youngest of nine children, raised on a tulip farm beside the Midford River.

Learning came easily. She excelled at school and showed distinct aptitude for science in the eighth grade. She was determined to be a doctor before age thirty.

The entrance to medical schools is fiercely guarded. Many knock, but few are allowed to enter. Marilyn passed the admission test with ease. She showed incredible aptitude for analytical thinking and exhibited superior communication skills. A smart doctor with a good bedside manner, she would be every patient's dream.

On February 13, 1963, the door to her future slammed shut.

"Miss Vanderberg, I'll see you in my office at 10:00 a.m. precisely."

Ralston Horvath was not popular, a dour man with a sallow face and dark circles around his eyes. He enjoyed his task of investigation and punishment altogether too much.

Marilyn waited quietly on a high-backed oak bench in the hallway. Behind smudged glass panels, Horvath was engaged in animated discussion with other staff members. She strained for voices, but doors to deans' offices are unusually soundproof.

Then, Dean Horvath ushered her into the sentencing room. "It has been brought to my attention that you are 'in the family way,' Miss Vanderberg. It is my responsibility to uphold the student code of conduct at this institution, and I intend to discharge my responsibility. A decision has been made to expel you immediately."

"I was raped, sir. If Vincent's family wasn't so prominent, he'd be up on charges right now."

"That is a matter to be handled by the courts, young lady. I must make decisions on this campus based on the evidence before me. You are no longer enrolled here. Good-bye, Miss Vanderberg."

Marilyn never married. She raised her daughter and pursued a career in the travel industry, retiring four years ago.

Now this letter.

Marilyn's choices are limited. There is only one constructive thing she can do now. After reading his request for the fifth time, she reaches a decision. Painfully, by return mail, she squeezes out forgiveness for the old man. He's released. And so is she.

*****

Ten months later, Marilyn receives a call from her granddaughter Melissa, shrieking on the phone, "Grandma, I'm going to med school!"

Melissa calms down eventually and explains what's happened. "You know how badly I've always wanted to be a doctor. I passed the admission test, no problem. Mom and Dad just didn't have the money to help me. I've been turned down for five scholarships. I gave up. Then this unexpected letter today."

"Who's it from, dear?"

"Some private foundation just awarded me a bursary for full tuition. Have you ever heard of the Ralston Horvath Memorial Foundation, Grandma? The letter says I'm their first recipient."

Truth in a beer can

Lana is waiting on the other side of the galvanized steel wall when "Rat" Peterson opens the gate at 8:00 a.m.

She's not sure about this skinny kid in the filthy white NASCAR T-shirt. His hands are permanently black. Straggly blond hair is jammed under a greasy red welder's hat.

As a lab tech, she works in a world of cleanliness and order.

Rat's world is full of metal skeletons. All he's known since grade nine is yanking parts, draining tanks and stacking car frames. He is paid minimum wage in the auto salvage yard, with the bonus of keeping anything he finds in the wrecks.

Lana steps forward, sidestepping a pool of red transmission oil. "I'm looking for a gold Chevy Suburban, towed here yesterday."

"I hope you're lookin' for rear end parts, lady. Nothin' left of the front end of that one. Got whacked real good."

Lana speaks slowly as she follows him to the far corner of the yard. "I need to look through that Suburban. My grandfather died in it."

Rat wipes his right hand on the back of his grimy jeans and offers it to her gently. "I figured somebody died in there. I'm awful sorry."

Archie's Suburban is sitting on blocks. Someone has already removed the two back doors. "Blood" is scribbled in yellow marker across the only window left on the driver's side.

Lana stops ten feet from the truck. She becomes unsteady at the sight of the mangled metal that took her grandpa.

Finally, she asks, "Was there alcohol involved?"

Rat scratches his head. "Yeah, I think so. Found a vodka bottle in the other car and some beer can thingy in this one."

Abruptly, she turns and walks back quickly towards the gate. She calls back, "That's all I needed to know. Thanks very much."

He calls after her. "Wait, lady. I don't think it was a real beer. There was something rattling in the can. I didn't get a chance to check it out. Was busy yesterday."

Lana turns around. "Did it smell like booze in his truck?"

"Don't think so," he answers.

Archie Coleman fought the bottle all his life. His family fully expected him to die drunk in a car wreck. His wife finally threw him out. Her parting words: "You won't see me again until you prove you're sober."

The family hadn't heard from him in two years.

The police told Lana that Archie died in a head-on collision on the highway about a mile from her grandmother's house.

Lana presses the salvage yard kid. "Show me what you found in the truck. I need to see everything."

Rat gets defensive. "There was just some loose change, a couple of maps and that can. I get to keep everything I find in these wrecks. If there's money in that can, it's mine."

Inside the yard shack, he digs through his loot pile. Retrieving what looks like a Budweiser can, he shakes it for Lana's benefit. Something rattles inside.

She looks at it carefully and then recognizes what it is. They're sold on TV: decoy cans, designed to hide valuables. She spins off the top.

Inside, she finds her grandpa's wedding ring and a small white envelope. Tucked in the envelope is a copy of the *12 Steps of Alcoholics Anonymous*, signed nine months earlier, and a photo of her grandmother. Lana is stunned. Her grandfather had finally found a way to replace the demons of the beer can with true treasure.

Rat watches her face. "Lady, I done pretty good lately. You can keep the can."

The germs will eat your sandwich

"Meep-meep, meep-meep." The roadrunner horn draws a crowd to Pavlov's Quick-Bite, the local lunch wagon. It's 11:55.

Like ants drawn to sugar, they form a crooked line, necks craned to see the daily specials on the side of the big, red van.

Forklift operators in green coveralls. Office girls in skirts and heels. Security guards in black uniforms.

Virginia's lunch menu lures them: roasted turkey breast with provolone cheese on crusty French bread; tangy tomato soup with basil; giant "rocko-choco" cookies; fresh-brewed Italian coffee.

She has been in the business twenty years and knows what sells.

Even though Virginia feeds hundreds every week and even counsels a few broken hearts in her lunch line-up, she doesn't feel fulfilled.

She questions her sister on the phone. "I'm over fifty and still driving a lousy lunch wagon. I barely earn enough to live on. What good am I?"

On her way out of the Silverwood industrial complex, she makes an unscheduled stop beside the entrance sign. There are no workers there. The sound of her horn brings a little boy from the rundown trailer park next door. The child is shy and dirty. Not filthy like a street bum, but stale-smelling. His hair is unwashed, and his Sponge Bob T-shirt is ketchup-stained. He's wearing yellow women's sandals with the Velcro straps wrapped twice around his ankles.

Virginia takes a Styrofoam container from the fridge and offers it to him.

A timid, sticky hand reaches for the chicken sandwich and vegetable soup. "Thanks, Aunty."

Then he disappears through a hole in the fence.

For the past month, Cody has been her project child, like the ones you sponsor in Africa. One day he even allowed her to wipe his face.

"If we don't clean around your mouth, the germs will eat some of your sandwich, and you won't get as much."

Who is this kid, and why is he hungry?

Cody is six, the only son of Lori Winslow. She's followed the family business of collecting welfare benefits and knows nothing else. Her problem is gambling—not the casino, but lotteries and the bingo hall. Her son's been raised by a seventeen-inch RCA color TV.

She tells Cody they'll buy a big white house with a swimming pool and a fenced yard for his new golden retriever puppy. The next ticket will be the big winner. The jackpot is nine million.

It's Friday noon. Cody's not at the Silverwood entrance today. Instead, there's a thirty-something woman leaning against the sign, weeping uncontrollably. "Cody's gone. I know you feed him sometimes. Have you seen my son?"

All weekend, rescue teams search for Cody. TV news crews follow the story. Lori pleads for his safe return.

Monday morning the "meep-meep" horn sounds at the Cascade sawmill on the far side of town. Ten mill workers grab their lunches. As Virginia closes the window to leave, she spots two little feet in women's sandals hobbling toward her behind a logging truck. She steps out and rushes to him.

"Aunty, I heard your 'meep-meep,' and I ran as fast as I could. I don't know how to get home. I'm so hungry."

The news feature draws city-wide attention. The next day, a reporter secretly follows Virginia, searching for the rest of the story.

The news at six shows her lunch wagon making three more "unscheduled stops" that day. Irish stew for a ninety-one-year-old man living in an abandoned guardhouse on the docks. Five loaves of multi-grain bread for an immigrant family taking shelter in a warehouse. Meat scraps over the fence for a skinny Rottweiler guarding a towing compound.

"We believe that this is a woman who has found true fulfilment in life," says the reporter.

All of the newsroom reporters and staff step in front of the cameras and applaud.

Grease pencil

"My father died six months ago and left me with nothing."

Hedy Rogers is a forty-three-year-old cashier at Sullivan's Supermarket. She's on a break, chatting with several other cashiers.

"My husband took off and left me with nothing but bills, and now I have nothing from my dad. I'll have to work till I'm eighty. I was hoping Dad would leave me at least something." Hedy looks at the others for reassurance, but none is offered.

"I think you're being too hard on your father," says a young cashier. "Did you think he should slave all his life, just to leave you a bundle you didn't work for?"

Hedy hasn't talked much about her father since his death, but she needs to speak. "He was a good father in some ways, but he was always cheap and secretive about his money. He haggled over everything he bought and came home with day-old bread, bruised apples and cracked eggs."

She looks down. "He was from the old country. I think his family lost everything in the war. He didn't trust banks or the government."

"Your dad was always friendly when he came into the store," comments another co-worker. "He was always joking about the outrageous prices, and he always wore that old, brown tweed hat. Did he only have one?"

"I told you he was cheap," Hedy replies. "He married late and was almost forty when I was born. Mom died when I was in my twenties. He lived much of his life alone. Why couldn't he have saved any money? We always rented, never owned a house."

"What was he like when you were growing up?" the co-worker asks.

Hedy looks at her watch. "I'll give you the short version. The Gaborsky home was a two-bedroom apartment with secondhand sofas. There was homemade wine in green bottles under my parents' bed and fresh brown bread and pork sausages on Saturdays. Love? He adored my mother Lena. He was never the same after she died. But I don't know if he loved me. He never said so."

"What did he say when your husband left you?"

"Dad wanted to kill him. He said he couldn't understand how a man could walk out on his family."

The break is over.

Hedy's voice catches. "Thanks for listening. I still feel cheated and abandoned. I guess I'm really on my own now."

Hedy touches up her makeup, puts on her "customer care" face and prepares for the line-up at checkout number six.

Next Saturday morning, Hedy's phone wakes her.

"Hallo, Hedy. Is Igor Mirkovic. I am fawder's friend. Can you come my home today? I give sometink for you."

She's in his kitchen by nine.

"Velcome my home, Hedy." Igor places a metal box on the table. "I know vell your fawder Ivan. Ve play on streets in old country. He told me I am to waiting six monts after he is died to give it you. Not trust govermant."

There is a letter inside the box:
Mine Hedy.

I was born and growing up in Krakow. I spend 56 years in Canada. I been butcher 40 years. I liked very much my job. Now, butcher shop I change for heaven and your mother Lena. You really good woman. I leaving you all mine life saved. Use wisely. I being proud of my Hedy.

Loving Papa

The metal box contains rectangular packages, neatly wrapped in brown butcher's paper. Each is labeled and dated with a grease pencil, some going back forty years: $161,000.

Not sad enough

"Connie, it's Mom. I can't find Patty. She's not answering her cell phone."

Mother catches her breath. "I just saw it on TV. The KPXG News plane crashed on the south slope of Mount Montez. They're talking about incinerated wreckage and names being withheld pending notification of next of kin. Andy is their only pilot. We've got to find her before she hears it on the news!"

Patty Kovacs will hear no news. She's on a two-day mountain hike with friends in Montez National Park. As credit manager for Fletcher Financial Group, she carries considerable stress. She insists the mountain air purifies her brain.

Her husband usually checks on her when she's hiking. The red-and-white Cessna circles, he tips its wings, Patty waves, and Andy Kovacs goes back to work as the "News Eagle" pilot for KPXG News.

She doesn't see him this morning, on the side of the mountain she's on, but doesn't worry. He must be following a breaking story. She's wrong.

Five hundred attend his memorial service at the end of the week. No casket. Flowers, candles and a large wooden easel with a photo of Andy in the cockpit, headset on, the city sprawled out below him.

Patty is strong at the funeral. She comforts her family and shows little emotion. She delivers the eulogy, unusual for a new widow.

Her mother encourages her to grieve. "It's all right to cry, sweetheart. Let it out. It's healthy."

Instead, Patty chats with guests and absorbs stories about her late husband.

Two days later, she's back at work.

Within a month, she's dealt with all the "details" of her husband's death. His new Toyota 4X4 is sold. She always disliked making his vehicle payments. "We don't need debt, Andy."

She settles his life insurance claim and pays off their mortgage. Andy disappears from their accounts.

Her sisters are suspicious. Her mother is worried. Her daughter is just not sad enough.

Patty responds, "Don't worry about me. I'm coping with things in my own way. I'm trying to keep busy. Andy and I talked about this when we married. Flying is risky."

A colleague from work spots her at the airport in the Wings and Prop Café with the new pilot for KPXG News. Was something going on before?

December is coming. Christmas time and what would have been Andy's fortieth birthday in the same month. It will be difficult for her.

Her sisters strategize. "We need to keep her busy. We'll meet for dinner, early, on the 14th. That way, we'll keep her mind off his birthday all evening."

Patty is not at work on the 14th when they call. She doesn't answer her cell phone.

Her sisters use the house keys she left them for emergencies. They go from room to room. Everything is in perfect order. Connie opens the door to Andy's office last. Unopened aviation mail from months ago. His brown leather flying jacket draped over the back of his chair. The brass propeller clock, a gift from his father, ticking faithfully on his desk. His first private pilot's license, in a black drugstore frame.

On a small table next to the window, her love for Andy is etched on a twelve-inch chocolate birthday cake. The tail of his Cessna, his aviator glasses and the altimeter he watched every day are perfectly replicated in colored frosting.

"Happy 40th, Andy. I'm yours forever."

Connie panics. "I'm trying her cell one more time!"

Patty finally answers: "I'm just out walking..."

Then the call breaks up. Cell phone service is terrible on the south slopes of Mount Montez.

Rendezvous at the Owl's Nest Motel

"The sign says 'No Vacancy.' Can't you read? Place is full up till Sunday. We only do weeklies now."

The overweight desk clerk in a sweat-stained green ball cap goes back to reading his wrestling magazine.

"But I drove three hundred miles to stay here. I need a room near the pool. I'll pay extra."

At the word "extra," the desk clerk struggles to his feet.

"For an extra hundred a week, I'll get you into number eleven, right beside the pool. Pool ain't got no water no more, though."

George Collins, sixty-one, is checking into the Owl's Nest Motel due to a doctor's diagnosis. Cancer. Three to six months left.

Yesterday morning, he stopped at the brown cedar church where he and Lucille were married thirty-eight years ago. Yesterday afternoon, he walked down Walnut Avenue, where they bought their first house and raised their boys. After that, he parked his beat-up Chevy van in the Melville Elementary School parking lot and relived the times he walked five-year-old Aaron through those doors to kindergarten. Now, Aaron's a bank manager.

The clerk hands George a worn brass key with a red plastic tag. "If you're thinkin' of leavin' early, there ain't no refunds."

George turns the key. The rundown room smells like body odor and beer.

At 11:00 p.m., he shuts off the snowy TV and slides into the patched green vinyl recliner by the window. He caresses a chipped mug of room-temperature Jack Daniels. The flashing red neon of the "No Vacancy" sign casts its mark over the soiled wool army blanket covering the sagging bed.

Memories of family vacations flood over him. Every August, they would pack up the kids in their wood-grain station wagon and head north to the Owl's Nest. It was new then.

Their sons would splash in the heated pool till well after dark. Then they'd tiptoe back to the room, wrinkled and shivering. He'd wrap them in fresh white motel towels while Lucille fixed hot chocolate and salty popcorn. Halfway through one of his famous "Billy Bear stories," they'd all be flaked out on the chenille bedspreads.

Then he'd take Lucille's hand, and they'd sit on white metal patio chairs watching the moon through the Ponderosa pines.

George Collins had a loving wife, three sons and grandchildren. He abandoned them many years ago to live with the bottle. Now, with bulging eyes and a grayish-yellow complexion, he's sitting in a cheap motel room thinking about the end.

When he tried to contact his family about his cancer, nobody replied.

George asked the desk clerk for writing paper. Instead, he sold him old motel postcards, four for a dollar.

He writes four separate messages. "I'm saying goodbye. I'm sorry."

This trip has been a poor substitute for the things he threw away.

Three months later, his obituary reads: "George A. Collins, sixty-one, of Marksville, a diesel mechanic, died Sunday in hospital. Arrangements by Cedar Hills Mortuary. No service."

The next morning, a tall, balding man in a navy business suit enters the reception area of the mortuary. "I'm Aaron Collins. Have you disposed of the body of my father George yet?"

A funeral director in the office overhears and comes to reception. "The cremation is scheduled for this afternoon. Would you like to see your father?"

"No!" he replies emphatically. "I swore I would never attend that man's funeral. I said my goodbyes many years ago."

"Then why have you come?"

Aaron holds up a crumpled postcard. "Could you put this with my father's body?"

In black ink on the front of the postcard are scrawled the words: "Dad, thanks for the Owl's Nest memories. We had good times then."

He's sold

Dean Potter has never been known as a success.

His upholstery repair business has paid the family bills for thirty years. He has faithfully purchased government bonds as a savings plan, but, at sixty-one, he's still a nobody.

Then, while repairing a silk cushion for a wealthy customer, he overhears her husband's phone conversation: "I'm dumping my shares in that new Crossley Country Club. Need the cash for a mining deal. Two hundred grand gives a guy Class A shares. Know anybody for them?"

Dean has always been curious about rich people's "insider deals."

Timidly, he asks the husband, "Would the country club investment be a good thing for me in my retirement?"

The entrepreneur assures him, "People with money will always golf. Half the memberships are already sold. Besides, owners get big tax breaks. You can't lose."

As Dean drives out through the customer's iron security gates, he calls his wife Loretta. "I've found a deal that will put us into retirement with some class. I'm sick of being the guy you call to fix your cushions."

She's puzzled by how he's acting lately—impulsive, like a squirrel getting ready for winter. "I know you'll get some good advice, honey. That's our life savings you're talking about."

The next day, Dean rents a silver Lincoln and drives to the country club. An attractive marketing woman tours him around the clubhouse, manicured fairways and future home sites.

He's sold.

Without getting any financial advice or telling his wife, he goes to the bank, cashes in his bonds and invests in the new Crossley Country Club.

Immediately, he's appointed to the club's "board of governors" and is invited to their next business meeting on Friday afternoon.

That night, Dean swaggers into the kitchen. "I made the deal, honey. You can quit your job. Once in a while, a guy gets a lucky break."

Loretta's excited. He's always made good choices for them.

Friday's meeting is in the owners' private lounge. He's surprised to see a number of sour-faced local contractors at the table along with the board members.

The club president addresses the group. "I'd like to welcome Mr. Potter. He comes highly recommended by an original investor who found other financial opportunities."

The group applauds halfheartedly.

"Hopefully, Mr. Potter, you will be able to help us negotiate through the tight financial position we currently find ourselves in. What is your background, sir?"

"Upholstery."

"Import-export?"

"No, sewing up rips in sofas and chairs."

"Really? How did you manage to do so well? Did you franchise nationwide?"

176

"No," Dean replies. "I worked from my garage and saved my money. Are you telling me things aren't going well?"

"We're on the verge of bankruptcy, Mr. Potter. Membership sales have dried up. We can't pay our debts. The contractors might get fifty cents on the dollar. I was under the impression from our former investor that you had the financial strength to shore up the project while we launched another aggressive marketing campaign. Is that not the case?"

Dean excuses himself, rushes down the hall to the men's room and retches. He looks in the mirror as he splashes water on his face. Wrinkles, thinning hair. He has run out of time.

He can't go home. He sits alone in a downtown cafe, nursing a lukewarm black coffee, double sugar.

At 10:00 p.m., he finally calls Loretta. He has never lied to his wife, and he isn't about to start now.

"Honey, I messed up. I don't know how I'll ever make it up to you."

Quietly, she responds. "I already know. Your accountant called the house looking for you. The bank apparently called him. He told me you made a mistake with the paperwork and the deal to buy the country club shares didn't go through. I know how upset you must be."

Left hand over right

It's 5:55 p.m. Fletcher's Jewelry closes in five minutes.

Emily's alone.

The front door opens. Emily doesn't want any new customers. She's got a date tonight.

A woman wearing a brown raincoat enters the store and says timidly, "I'd like to buy a ring."

"Not tonight," Emily thinks. "I can't be late."

This will be her first date with Darren, a medical student she met recently. She's promised to meet him in an hour, and there's barely enough time to get ready as it is.

"We're closing now, ma'am."

"Oh, I'm so sorry to trouble you," replies the woman. "I've been at the nursing home most of the day with my husband."

Emily slips on her jacket. "I'd like to help you, but I have an appointment."

Tears well up in the old woman's weary blue eyes. "I want to give him this before he goes."

She unties a white handkerchief and lays it on the counter. The light sparkles on a tiny diamond.

"It's from my engagement ring. Even though Henry gave me a new one for our fiftieth, it's still precious because it reminds me of the wonderful man who saved up for a whole year to buy it for me. He slipped it on my finger fifty-six years ago as we walked along the beach. That's the first time I let him kiss me.

178

I was so shy. Can you put this diamond in a new wedding band for him?"

How can Emily say no? She slips off her jacket and locks the door. "Would he like yellow gold?"

The elderly woman looks through the selection carefully. Finally, she says, "I'll take the last one on the right. It looks manly."

As she unlocks the door for her departing customer, Emily thinks, "Fifty-six years. I hope I find a man like that someday."

Emily is late for her date. She explains that an important client came in just before closing. Darren says nothing.

She feels comfortable with Darren, but is he the right man? What's he really thinking?

After their date, she doesn't hear from him for over two weeks. She's confused.

Unexpectedly, he calls her at work. "Can you meet me for dinner at The Beach House restaurant?"

She's not sure if she should. Why hasn't he called her sooner?

Still uncertain, she accepts.

Emily arrives at the restaurant right on time. Darren's not there. Embarrassed, she waits twenty minutes.

He finally arrives, out of breath. "Sorry I'm late, Emily. I'm doing my practicum at a nursing home. I just witnessed an amazing story. I couldn't leave."

"A story?"

"I'll tell you later this evening."

After dinner, he suggests a walk on the beach. They stroll in silence.

Finally, he begins. "There's an older gentleman in Room 407. His wife comes every day to sit with him. She holds his hand for hours and just looks at him. He

179

doesn't seem to recognize her. This afternoon, she brought in a man's ring wrapped in a handkerchief. She told me the band was new but the diamond was from her original engagement ring."

Darren struggles with his words, but continues. "As his wife slipped the ring on his finger, the old man stirred and held his arms open for her. They hugged. I noticed the ring was too loose, so I taped it up for them. That's why I was late."

During the next hour, Darren kisses Emily on the beach, and the gentleman in Room 407 passes away with his wife at his side.

The nurse carefully places the elderly man's hands, left over right.

The tiny diamond sparkles under the fluorescent light.

The wife touches the diamond tenderly and then nods her approval for the nurse to cover him.

Girls in these situations

"Grandma, who was your birth mother?" Cassie asks. "Did you have any sisters?"

"I don't know, dear," Vivian replies. "You weren't told those things back in the thirties. Adopted children were expected to be grateful that a good family took them in and not ask unnecessary questions."

Cassie Rowlandson is a twenty-four-year-old college student, fascinated with family history. She has set her sights on finding out who her biological great-grandmother was. But opening the door to the past might come with consequences. Is it worth the risk?

"When did you know you were adopted, Grandma?"

"My classmates in elementary school called me 'Blackie' because of my dark hair. My three brothers had blue eyes and blond hair. When I asked my mother why I was different, she told me I was their special girl. They had gone all the way to the city to fetch me when I was a baby."

"Did you fit in with your adopted family?" Cassie asks.

"I felt secure as a child. They were very kind to me. Secretly, I always longed for a sister." Vivian realizes this may sound ungrateful and stops. "I'm satisfied with the way I was raised. Why don't we just leave well enough alone?"

As Cassie leaves, her determination builds. She'll start her research on the Internet. Grandma says she was born at Toronto General Hospital.

Cassie discovers that adoption disclosure laws are changing rapidly. Sealed adoption records are being opened. Mothers who gave up children for adoption many years ago are being identified.

Aunty Rose finds out what she's doing. "Stop this nonsense immediately. Why are you so concerned about the identity of someone your grandmother never knew who has long since passed away? Lives will be shattered if you open this Pandora's box. Get back to your schoolwork and leave the past in the past."

Fuel on the fire...Now Cassie really digs in.

She searches birth and adoption records for April 1936. Some things match perfectly. Some information is unclear. She probes deeper.

Several months later, Cassie knows the entire history. Should she tell her family?

"Grandma, I've discovered things you need to know. You can keep it to yourself if you wish, but I love you too much to keep it a secret any longer."

Vivian is uncertain, afraid the truth may change her life. "Many nights, I've lain awake wondering what my mother's face looked like. Dark hair and brown eyes like me? Was she able to name me, or did someone else make that choice? But I'm older now, Cassie. Maybe it's better you don't tell me. Do you think it's really that important?"

"Yes," insists her granddaughter. "Your birth mother's name was Virginia Knowlton. She was the daughter of a prominent prairie politician. Her unwanted pregnancy caused the family shame and embarrassment, so they sent her to the city to folks who dealt with girls in these situations. She was able to return after relinquishing her child, supposedly having gone to secretarial school for a year."

Cassie continues. "Your mother gave birth on April 17, 1936. Vital Statistics shows a death certificate for her less than two weeks later, on April, 30 1936. Surviving relatives in her family believe it was suicide."

Vivian buries her face in her hands.

Cassie kneels beside her. "Grandma, there's more. Your mother gave birth to two babies on April 17, 1936. She named them Vivian and Violet. Twin babies going for adoption were often separated back then. Your sister Violet is living in Victoria."

Take Timmy too

Monica sets down a round of drinks for table number five and bursts into tears.

"Whatsa matter?"

These folks are regulars, so she tells them. "Colin's applying for custody of my kids. Claims I'm an unfit mother."

A patron who has consumed more than a few "pink ladies" offers to write a letter of recommendation. "I'll tell 'em you've never ripped me off on a drink in three years!"

Monica holds out a wrinkled legal notice to a group of construction workers at the next table. "Any of you guys ever go through a custody thing? Can they really take my kids away?"

The foreman takes the letter.

"This is serious, Monica. Your ex wants sole custody of your kids. He's started legal proceedings claiming you aren't fit to parent." He reads out the names: "Sarah Elizabeth Jenkins, Megan Victoria Jenkins, Breanna Marie Jenkins."

Monica gasps. "But I've got four kids. Doesn't he want Timmy?"

She reads the notice carefully, twice. Nowhere is Timmy mentioned.

Her son just turned thirteen. He was always a bit different. Her husband gave up trying to get him into sports years ago. Timmy gave up easily and embarrassed the team and his father.

But he is brilliant in math and was an expert on sharks at age ten, reciting their names and feeding patterns. Timmy would be happy to stay in his room and draw pictures of sharks all day if Monica let him.

Colin and Monica Jenkins split up two years ago. The divorce proceedings were bitter, and painful for the children.

Colin has taken a different job and is now doing well financially. He is meticulous and orderly and passionate about diet, health and fitness. His record of fulfilling his financial obligations and keeping his "parenting time" schedule with the children is impeccable. This will undoubtedly help him in court.

Monica's intentions are good, but her reputation is questionable. She's known to drink and socialize with men she meets at the lounge where she works. She leaves many parenting responsibilities to her mother and father, who live two blocks from her home.

Colin intimidates Monica on the phone. "You'll have no chance in court. My lawyer will bring up the time you were suspected of drunk driving two years ago. Why don't you just agree to my application for custody now and get it over with?"

Faced with losing her children, Monica quits her job and goes back to school. Her parents gladly look after the kids while she gets her life in order and prepares for her court date.

She has no lawyer. The judge hearing the application asks her if she wishes to speak.

She reads from a sheet of lined paper. "No one could ever love their children more than me. I made a lot of mistakes, but I'm taking steps to change my life." She dabs at her eyes and has trouble continuing. "If you decide I'm an unfit mother and Colin should get the girls, I think he should take Timmy too. My son deserves to be raised properly and to be with his sisters. Please let me keep all my children or let Colin raise them all. I love them too much to see them split up."

The judge's decision is rendered two weeks later: "Joint custody of the four children is awarded to Monica Burrows and her parents, Edward and Joyce Burrows. The biological father, Colin Jenkins, will retain the right to visit the children at reasonable and proper times."

Monica tearfully embraces her parents.

The judge continues. "My decision is based on the fact that a father who chooses not to parent a child who exhibits signs of autism is not a fit parent."

Rilla's recliner

"Look, lady, I can't squish this thing like a rubber ball to make it fit through your skinny doorway. Recliners have wooden frames and steel hinges. They don't squish."

Rilla Tompkin's new green velour recliner is wedged halfway into the doorway of her apartment. It's just too wide to go through.

The frustrated delivery driver and his helper have tried every possible tilt and angle to get it in. They've rotated it sideways and stood it on end, yet nothing's worked.

Rilla is inside her apartment wringing her hands. "I don't know what to do. I paid for it with my Christmas money, and Benny the salesman said he would deliver it for free. Mother's coming on the bus tomorrow at two o'clock and needs a place to sleep sitting up because she's short of breath. Everything else is ready. Are you sure you can't get it through my door?"

"Got a chainsaw, lady?" The delivery men yank the recliner back out into the hallway.

Rilla tugs her brown sweater around her shoulders and shuffles out into the hall. She says quietly, "Leave it outside my door then. I'll just have to wait for a miracle. Do you believe in miracles?"

"Miracles!" The older one snorts as they head for the sidewalk. "Lady's gone wacko...That thing ain't never goin' in there."

Rilla steps back toward her apartment, glancing anxiously at her new recliner now shoved up against the stairwell on the ground floor of the Cityview Apartments.

Two of the kids from the third floor are banging down the stairs. One has a bat and ball. "Throwin' that chair out, lady?" he asks.

"No. I'm waiting for a miracle."

She can hear them laughing as they slam the steel door leading to the alley.

Two months ago, she started preparing a spot next to the front window for the new recliner. A white-painted side table and a tall brass lamp with an energy-saver bulb sit in place next to where the chair will go. A colorful patchwork quilt lies folded on the windowsill.

Rilla's stepfather died this year and finally released her mother from twenty years of virtual slavery. A domineering man, he demanded constant service, even though her mother's health was poor and she was seriously overweight.

Rilla, forty-five, is overweight as well and wasn't welcome in her stepfather's home. He said she was lazy and should get a better job. Asthma wasn't a good enough excuse.

So, she lived by herself in a low-income apartment four hundred miles from them. She missed her mother terribly. They wrote to each other every week. Now, her mother has agreed to live with her.

There's a sharp rap on her door. She peeks through the peephole. It's the building manager with a battered aluminum clipboard. He shouts through the door, "Rilla, get that big chair moved immediately, or it'll be out in the alley. Fire hazard!"

She opens the door a crack and looks at him with pleading eyes. "Could you just give me a few hours? My mother's coming, and I'm waiting for a miracle."

"If miracles happened, none of us'd be stuck in this dump," he snarls.

Before he can say another word, there is a terrible crash in Rilla's apartment. Shattered glass spreads across the shiny vinyl floor, and a scuffed baseball rolls slowly to a stop near the doorway. She hears boys' voices and feels the cool wind invading her apartment.

Within an hour, the glass company truck arrives. They remove her damaged front window. It's sixty inches wide and forty-eight inches high—more than enough room to shove her new recliner through.

Sophia sacrificed for an antique watch

"Sophia, please sit down." The hotel manager motions to a wooden chair against the wall in his office. "Our guests in Suite 1269 have something to ask you."

Sophia smooths her blue apron, smiles at the guests and folds her hands in her lap. "Are you enjoying your suite?" she asks warmly. "Have I brought you enough towels?"

Daphne Bassett, a heavyset, middle-aged woman with spiky gray hair, rises from a leather chair, shoves her index finger at Sophia and says angrily, "My mother's watch is gone. Where is it?"

Sophia shrinks back. "I haven't seen a watch in your suite. Can I help you look for it?"

Frank Bassett moves next to his wife. He's a tall, bony man with yellowish-gray hair.

He lowers his head to make direct eye contact with Sophia. "We travel all over the world and stay in five-star hotels. The thought never crosses our mind that we should be concerned about the integrity of the staff."

The hotel manager reaches for a notepad. "Mrs. Bassett, can you describe the watch?"

Daphne pulls out a wrinkled photo of a well-dressed older woman reaching for a glass of champagne. She's wearing a gold watch.

"It's an antique, eighteen-karat gold Patek Philippe, made in Switzerland. My mother gave it to me on her deathbed." She glares at Sophia. "Now where have you hidden it?"

Sophia lifts her apron to her face and sobs. "I would jump from your balcony before I would touch your possessions."

She's a petite forty-year-old with ivory skin and dark, braided hair tucked under a hairnet. For thirteen years, she has worn this hotel's housekeeping uniform. Because of her flawless record, she was recently assigned to the exclusive 12th floor suites.

Wealthier guests. Bigger tips.

But the work is still the same--ten suites per day. Scrubbing strangers' tubs with orange-scented cleansers and folding the tips of their toilet paper rolls into neat triangles.

Sophia is the sole provider for her family. Her husband Leo is a pale-faced, overweight fifty-year-old in baggy, gray sweatpants who seldom leaves his vinyl recliner. Severe depression has chained him to the sports channel.

Two years ago, on the strength of her job history, she took out a mortgage and purchased a two-bedroom apartment. She's struggling to make the payments. She's trying to save enough to send her six-foot-seven son Brett to college, so he can pursue his dream of playing basketball.

The hotel manager stands.

"Sophia, please give me your passkey."

He turns to the guests. "Mr. and Mrs. Bassett, our security staff will investigate this matter immediately. We will not rest until you are satisfied."

Sophia takes the bus home, alone. Housekeeping staff from the lower floors are delighted to finish her suites.

At 3:30, her son Brett bursts into the hotel manager's office. "My mother won't stop crying. She won't talk. What happened?"

"A piece of jewelry is missing."

"I'll work for you for free. I'll do anything for her. I'll give up basketball."

"Go home, son. I'll want to talk to your mother later."

At nine o'clock the following morning, Daphne Bassett answers a knock on the door of Suite 1269. The hotel manager and two uniformed police officers are standing there.

"It's about time," she says. "Has that foolish woman confessed?"

The manager says, "Your room key, please. These officers want to talk to you. Our security staff contacted them seeking information. According to police records, your mother's gold watch seems to have a habit of hiding from you in expensive hotels."

At the same time, there's a knock on another door down the hall. A cheerful voice calls out, "Good morning! It's Sophia. Ready for housekeeping?"

Thinks he's John Lennon

Tina Barrett calls to her husband downstairs. "He's alive! I just saw Dane on TV. The news is showing a holiday dinner for the homeless. We've got to find him and call Elliott."

Dane is her forty-eight-year-old nephew who disappeared several years ago.

According to his father Elliott, who lives across the country, Dane's life has been a waste. "He never did any honest work. Spent all his time with that stupid guitar, dreamin' about bein' a songwriter."

Nevertheless, Uncle Jess and Aunt Tina always liked their long-haired nephew. He stayed with them several summers as a teenager. They knew he was desperate to get away from his domineering father. Dane was always helpful but never did get a summer job. He spent his days downstairs playing guitar, filling notebooks with music and lyrics.

Cautiously, Jess and Tina start their search in the hard-edged world of the homeless. They shouldn't be here. It's not safe.

"Have you seen Dane Barrett?" Jess shows an old photo. "He's late forties now, ponytail, plays the guitar."

A wino looks up from the brown paper bag he's squeezing. "You're talkin' 'bout that guy thinks he's John Lennon. He's probly sleepin' in the old van behind the hotel."

Dane lives in an unlicensed yellow Volkswagen bus. Sitting on a stool where the passenger seat used to be, he often entertains other homeless people with his latest songs, mostly about loss and life on the street. They all believe he'll be a big star someday.

Jess taps on the window. "Come home with us, Dane. Aunt Tina will cook you roast beef with mashed potatoes and gravy."

He grabs his guitar and joins them willingly.

Jess's phone call to his brother is awkward. "We found Dane. He's staying with us for a while."

Elliot's voice is cold. "I've always expected to get a call that he's dead. Don't give him any money. He's good for nothing."

Jess asks his brother the hard question. "Do you want to talk to your son?"

"Not really. After all these years, there's really nothing to say."

Elliott hangs up.

After a few days, Dane disappears again. They drive around looking, but there's no sign of him.

A year goes by. One Sunday morning, a police officer is at their door. "We found your name and address in one of his music notebooks."

Now, they must call Elliott. He's away, and it takes three days to reach him.

"I'm sorry, Elliott. Dane drowned last Saturday night."

"I'm not surprised," Elliott replies. His voice shows no sympathy. "He was probably high on drugs. Just send me the bill for the burial."

"You need to hear this, Elliott. Your son's story is big news across the country. They even played one of his songs on national TV."

Jess reads him the front page headline. "Homeless man saves baby, then sinks to his death."

Dane Barrett, forty-nine, was playing his guitar in the park when a speeding SUV jumped the curb, knocking a young mother pushing a baby stroller into the icy waters of the Westside River. Passersby pulled the mother out, but the baby disappeared. Barrett dove down numerous times and finally surfaced with the baby, still strapped into her stroller. He managed to pass her to those on shore before being swept away. The baby survived. Barrett's body was recovered an hour later under the Belmont Bridge.

"Elliott, we've been flooded with calls from the media wanting details about your son. They're calling him a hero. This morning, a music company called, wanting to buy the rights to everything he's ever written."

Ernie can't even give it back

"Hey, old man, buy us all a Coke and a bag of chips. My dad says you're loaded."

A group of school kids hanging around the gas station are taunting an elderly man filling up an old, gray Taurus wagon. It's pulling a battered white "truck box" trailer piled high with old children's bikes, tricycles and plastic "ride-em" toys.

Ernie Blitz used to be known around town as "the toy man." Since he retired as a farm machinery mechanic, he's spent all his time looking for bikes and toys at garage sales, fixing them up and giving them to needy families.

Now, he's known as Lucky Ernie.

As he leaves the gas station, he hears the kids jeering. "Cheapie! Hope the mice eat all your money!"

After he empties his trailer at his workshop, Ernie heads to a women's shelter to deliver a shiny, red tricycle with a new seat and white streamer handle grips.

When he arrives, everybody hangs around his car, looking sad but hopeful. Several women pass him handwritten notes. A young mother with a bruise on her cheek asks, "Could you help me out with my rent for three months?"

After he unloads the tricycle, the supervisor waits expectantly without thanking him as she usually does.

Ernie's life has been turned upside down since he won six million on a ticket he purchased for five dollars at the Lucky Lion Lotto Center in the mall.

He was on the front page of the local paper holding the oversized cheque. A tall, lanky man of seventy-three with a black cowboy hat and deep-set gray eyes. He was smiling underneath a sign that read "Congratulations, Lucky Ernie!"

Since then, nobody's treated him the same.

He used to buy his buddies coffee once in a while. Now his friend Tony gets huffy about it. "We don't need some mega-millionaire buying nothing for us. You go ahead and show off your money somewhere else."

Ernie replies, "What's wrong with you guys? I'm the same old Ernie."

"Then put up some money for our seniors' center, you cheapskate. You know it's shutting down if we don't raise the money."

Ernie walks out of the coffee shop and drives directly to the lottery office where he picked up his winnings.

He asks for the advisor who had counseled him before he went public. "Dora, I want to give it all back. I feel like a miser for not fixing everyone's money problems. It gnaws at me twenty-four hours a day."

He pulls out a checkbook. "Who do I make it out to?"

"Mr. Blitz, you can't give it back. You bought the ticket, and you claimed the money."

Ernie then drives to the office of his favorite charity. "I'm here to make a substantial donation."

The manager takes him into her office and closes the door. "Mr. Blitz, we thank you for your offer. You are a generous man, and heaven knows we need the money, but we won't be able to accept it. We counsel our clients against gambling, and it's our policy not to accept funds that are proceeds of lottery wins."

Ernie grits his teeth in frustration and stomps out of the office. On the sidewalk, he suddenly clutches his chest and slumps to the ground.

Ernie dies alone two days later.

His entire estate goes to a distant nephew known to be reckless with money.

On Saturday afternoon, the day of Ernie's funeral, the line-up at the Lucky Lion Lotto Center in the mall stretches out through the front doors. The jackpot for tonight's draw is estimated at twenty-eight million.

A promise to the granite

"Mrs. Haisley, please pull out the purple sweet williams you planted behind your gravestone. I didn't mind when you visited every week to look after things. But you haven't been here for a while."

"I'm sorry, Herb," says the tall, well-dressed widow. "I didn't plan to be so busy."

The caretaker turns away, continuing to spray toxic weed killer around the cemetery entrance gate.

With her head down, Loretta Haisley walks to the familiar plot.

She stands silently in front of the "side by side" grave marker she and her husband Bill chose for themselves. Five years ago, as she sat on his hospital bed, they decided on Glacier Mist polished granite with the words "Together Again" etched inside the symbol of a heart between their names.

Before they made their decision, Bill gently took her hand and whispered, "Are you sure you want to do this, sweetheart? I want you to be happy. Maybe you'll find someone else after I'm gone."

She turned to her husband of forty-three years and said, "You are my only man, Bill Haisley."

Now, Loretta steps back from their granite marker and walks towards the caretaker. With great difficulty, she asks, "How do you change a gravestone?"

Shaking his head, he replies coldly, "I have done it before when ordered to, but I never expected you would be one of those women who break their promises."

Loretta runs to her car in tears.

Six months ago, on a Saturday morning at the supermarket parking lot, her shopping cart rolled back and scratched the side of a silver Land Rover. She sat in her car, waiting for the owner, expecting the worst. When he returned, she confessed to the mishap.

To her surprise, he wasn't angry. "I'm Clyde," he said with an English accent. "Tiny scrape. Not to worry." His eyes were ice-blue, and some blond still showed through his gray hair. He was her age and had never married.

Loretta had never dreamed she could have feelings for another man, but Clyde is the reason for her question about the gravestone today.

Loretta thinks about Clyde. A retired executive. Used to having things done his way. Well-tailored clothes and a Rolex watch. She hears his words echoing in her ears: "Loretta, I love you, but I am not going to wait forever for you to make a decision. Make a commitment to marry me, or stop wasting my time."

She reasons with herself, "My vows with Bill only said, 'Till death do us part.' He said he wanted me to be happy after he was gone."

In turmoil, Loretta calls Clyde and asks to meet him at their favorite restaurant. When he arrives, he's immediately concerned. "What's troubling you, my love?"

"I can't marry you, Clyde. You deserve a woman who will give you her whole heart."

She turns her face towards the window. "Clyde, I made a promise to Bill that's written in stone."

He takes her hand. "We need to talk to somebody about this."

Twenty minutes later, they're standing in front of William Haisley's gravestone.

"Mr. Haisley," Clyde begins. "I am here because I want to marry your wife. I know Loretta was yours first, but you're not here now. It isn't fair for you to hold on to her anymore. I promise you that I will love her, take care of her and do everything that you would have done."

Clyde smiles at Loretta before turning back to the gravestone. "And when Loretta's time on this earth comes to a close, I vow to give her back to you. Her name will be with yours forever."

Good-for-nothing runt

"I'm sorry to hear about your father, Ms. Gibbins."

Hotel reception clerks are trained to spot the reason for the reservation. The registration card shows a forty per cent bereavement discount—a guest attending her elderly father's funeral.

Paula is exhausted. Up at 5:00 a.m., two plane changes and a lost bag to deal with.

This place looks expensive: teak reception desk, polished marble foyer and doormen in royal burgundy uniforms pushing brass luggage carts.

Paula resigns herself to spending a bundle. "Here goes a big chunk of my vacation money," she thinks.

Reluctantly, she offers her credit card and accepts her room key. Her Aunt Tillie has arranged the rooms for the funeral guests. Good taste—rich aunties can probably afford it.

Paula really doesn't want to be here. She almost didn't come to her father's funeral. Paula has never been close to him. He didn't talk much—just went to work at the butcher shop every morning, came home for supper, watched TV and went to bed. She knew he worked hard. They always had everything they needed.

Her friends' dads were normal. They would joke and tease and talk to the girls about almost anything, including boys. When Paula would ask for help or advice, her dad would respond with "Ask your mother."

He was distant. She often thought of him as her "stone statue dad," always there providing for them but never warm or nurturing. He gave her a generous allowance but no special "Daddy surprise gifts," not even at graduation.

She is disappointed with her father and believes she had an unhappy childhood because of him.

Paula is fifty and floundering with her personal relationships. She is attending this funeral because it is the right thing to do, not because she is heartbroken at the loss of a loving father.

A note under the door asks her to contact Aunt Tillie in Room 271. Will Paula join her for dinner?

Tillie is her classy aunt from Toronto. Paula adored her as a child. She always looked so elegant at family gatherings with her tailored outfits and Italian leather shoes.

Will she still be wearing Chanel No. 5?

They meet in the hotel restaurant at seven. "Order what you like, dear. My treat. Our waiter recommends the grilled king salmon with lemon dill vinaigrette."

Dinner is fabulous, just what Paula needed.

"Why was my dad so cold and distant, Aunt Tillie? I never felt close to him, no matter what I did."

"He was a good man, Paula. He always provided for your family."

"What was he like growing up? Tell me the truth. I need to know. Something was wrong, wasn't it?"

Aunt Tillie is hesitant. "It was your grandfather, Thomas. He was a cold and cruel man. Your father Elliott was a victim of harsh discipline. I guess I must tell you now that he's gone."

Aunt Tillie continues: "Your father's father was a stonemason by trade. He died when Elliott was nineteen. He was a big man, six-foot-two, with heavy black sideburns and an angry disposition. Father ignored the rest of us children but always bullied your dad, maybe because he was small as a teenager. Father would call him weak and worthless and beat him with a chunk of black leather harness for not stacking the rocks straight. I remember the night Elliott was tied with twine to the split rail fence and left in the rain. Father was yelling at him, 'I'll make a man out of you yet, you good-for-nothing runt.'"

Tillie's eyes fill with tears.

Paula is horrified. "Why did Grandma let this happen?"

"She had no control," Tillie replies. "Women had nothing to say back then. Your dad was hurt, shamed and humiliated by his father, and there was nothing she could do to stop it. Her heart was breaking for him. We heard her crying at night."

Tillie goes on. "It was abuse, plain and simple. Your grandfather Thomas would go to jail today for what he did to your father. Elliott was an amazing man, Paula, to be able to lead a normal life after the emotional and physical trauma he'd faced. Somehow, he covered his hurt and humiliation."

Aunt Tillie pauses for a while as if preparing for her grand finale.

"Do you know what's really amazing about your father, Paula? He broke the cycle of violence and abuse and didn't take it out on you. He was a good father, maybe not the warmest or the funniest, but he did well. I am so proud of my brother."

At the funeral, Paula approaches the microphone with several pages of hand-written notes. "I didn't plan to speak today, but I absolutely must pay tribute to a man I didn't really know..."

There's gold under the trailer in Appleton Acres

Bertie MacGregor wriggles through a narrow spot where the skirting has been pried open by a neighbor looking for his cat. The soil under the mobile home is damp, and wads of sagging insulation cling to her hair and shoulders as she crawls between boxes of empty wine bottles. She has a small garden shovel in one hand and a tiny purple penlight in the other.

Yesterday, the welfare lady was here. "Bertie, you'll have to move. You don't get enough money to be able to stay here by yourself anymore."

"Don't say that." Bertie covers her ears. "I don't want to live anywhere but here!"

"I'll find you a nice place, Bertie. Lots of your neighbors are moving too. You're not the only one."

Bertie has always lived with her mother in their "ten-by-fifty" trailer in Appleton Acres Mobile Home Park. Just over a year ago, her mother, diagnosed with Alzheimer's, was moved to a nursing home.

Bertie's gotten by, living mostly on fried wieners, eggs and cereal, but park management has just raised the monthly pad rental fees. "For sale" signs are going up in the front windows of many of her neighbors' trailers.

Bertie is forty and has never worked or had a boyfriend. She's short and heavy with creamy white skin, innocent brown eyes and a receding chin that disappears into her pudgy neck. She wears flowered cotton dresses and white wool sweaters. Bertie points and talks to the TV during her favorite programs. "I told you so. He's not a nice man. Why don't you listen?"

The actors are her friends. She wants to help them if she can.

Life was good when her mother was here. Every afternoon at three, Bertie would take her yellow, plastic change purse and head for the door. "Going for a cherry cola, Mother. Get you one too?"

The answer was always the same. "No, Bertie. You know I don't like pop. Remember, no talking to strangers."

Bertie's mother lived on welfare for twenty years after her husband left. She drank cheap red wine and watched TV sixteen hours a day. She always had just enough to pay the rent at the end of the month. Bertie's known nothing different. Her life has been TV, hot dogs and cold cherry cola. Her mother always told her not to worry about anything. "We've got gold under this trailer if we ever really need money."

Now, Bertie desperately needs the money to pay her rent, and she's gone under the trailer to dig it up.

But there is no gold. Bertie digs hopefully in different spots with her little shovel, but all she finds in the spot where she always imagined the gold would be is a mummified mouse with yellow, protruding teeth.

The welfare lady arrives to pick her up and notices the trailer door is open.

She calls out, "Bertie, I brought you a cherry cola."

Bertie sobs from under the trailer, "There's no gold."

Puzzled, the welfare lady bends down and peers under the trailer. As she does, a rusty cookie tin is dislodged from the insulation and bounces on the ground. Curious, she opens it. It contains an old newspaper clipping from twenty years ago: "Angus MacGregor leaves mineral fortune to extended family."

The welfare lady calls a department lawyer on her cell phone. A quick legal search shows a significant inheritance for Bertie's mother is still being held in trust. One of the conditions of the inheritance is that she be able to prove avoidance of alcohol for a minimum of one year.

She ponders a moment and asks the lawyer, "They don't serve alcohol in nursing homes, do they?"

"ME" in blue bubble letters

"This guy must want to get caught. You can still smell the spray paint!"

Lem Saunders, the gray-bearded janitor at Westview High School, is standing at the side door of the school gymnasium pointing at a basketball backboard dripping with fresh graffiti.

A pack of tenth-graders pass by, their ears plugged with earbuds. Some of them laugh. None of them offers to help clean up the mess.

They mystery graffiti artist, or "tagger," is the talk of the school. His graffiti signature is "ME" in scrawly, fluorescent blue bubble letters. He's already tagged the staff room door, the heating duct above the principal's office and the side of the pop machine by the girls' change room, all during school hours. Everybody's guessing where "ME" will show up next.

Joel Bailey, a skinny ninth-grader with a bulging black backpack, steps to the doorway beside Lem. "Art students must be pretty tall these days," he says with a smirk.

Lem's not in the mood for jokes this morning. "I can't keep up with my normal work plus clean up this graffiti every week."

Joel drops his backpack on the gym floor. Looking up, he says, "That's gotta be ten feet high. Do you want me to hold the ladder while you do your janitor eraser job?"

"Thank you, Joel," replies Lem. "You're a good kid, you know."

Joel hangs around the school a lot. Everybody assumes he comes from a troubled home and has nowhere to go. He doesn't do well in school and has no friends.

As Lem reaches the top rung with his can of solvent and a rag, the principal marches triumphantly through the door. "So you caught the social deviant, and now you're letting him get away with it. Is that it? Your duty is to bring him to my office immediately, not let him help with the cleanup. For the last thirty years, you've been too soft. Students don't respect weakness, Lem. I'll deal with this situation."

Turning to Joel, the principal snarls, "Get to my office!"

Lem glares defiantly from the top of the ladder. "I'm due for retirement, so I'll say what I feel. I've watched you ruin many kids in this school with your accusatory attitude. Why would a good kid like Joel do something like this? He's the only one who volunteered to help. All the other kids just walked by and laughed. Now, get back to your office, and let me do my job!"

The principal scowls at both of them but then slowly retreats to his office.

Lem Saunders retires three months later. His send-off retirement party is in the gym on a Friday afternoon.

The back wall is draped with a gigantic sheet of white paper. Mrs. Ferguson, the French teacher, takes the microphone. "For many years, Lem, you cleaned up graffiti in this school, along with other, unmentionable messes. We wish you some 'good graffiti' to take with you into your retirement."

During the party, students, staff and parents walk to the paper graffiti wall to record their memories of Lem Saunders with colorful felt markers.

Near the end of the party, Joel Bailey joins a group of parents at the wall. He draws a ladder and scribbles several lines. Then, unexpectedly, he pulls a spray can out of his jacket, and "ME" appears in scrawly, fluorescent blue bubble letters. The crowd gasps as the smell of paint spreads through the gym.

Joel turns toward Lem. "Mr. Saunders, I know I'm kicked out for good now, but I wanted you to know it was me."

"But why, Joel?"

"I needed the world to know that I exist. Other than my graffiti, you're the only one that ever made me feel that way."

If Grandpa dies, he gets the money

Jason's relationship with Miranda is based on deception.

He drives a black hybrid SUV. His platinum credit card buys her expensive outfits. It's not unusual for dozens of I-love-you roses to show up at the Salon de Roussel where she works as a makeup artist.

Miranda is beautiful, but she lives with her mother and younger sister in a tiny, low-rent apartment. Years ago, she made herself a promise: "I'll never marry a poor man like my Daddy."

A friend calls her at work. "You are so lucky, Miranda. I just spotted Jason's truck in front of Marsella's Jewelry. Are you expecting something?"

The truth is, Jason is living on credit, waiting for his share of the inheritance. His Grandpa Karl is near death.

Jason has a good job with Capital 5 Construction, but his wages don't cover what he's spending.

If Grandpa dies, he gets the money, and she'll never know. If Grandpa hangs on, he'll run out of credit, and the whole pretense will blow up in his face.

Miranda was always the "unreachable beauty." He's convinced she wouldn't go out with him if she knew the truth. But he's so close. He can't lose her now.

Creditors call him constantly on his cell phone. She thinks he's talking business.

There's trouble at work. His foreman yells, "Jason, what are you thinkin', buddy? You dropped that whole load of rock on the wrong side of the road. Get your head back on the job."

Jason can't stop thinking about his grandfather.

Finally, he goes to the hospital and tells him the whole story. "I can't imagine life without you, Grandpa, and I can't imagine life without Miranda. It's like I'm waiting for you to die to keep her happy."

The cancer has strangled Karl's booming voice. He whispers, "You're a big man for telling me, but I already knew. I can see you're trying to impress her. I once paid a guy five bucks to borrow his yellow Buick convertible to take your grandma to the fair."

Karl's voice is almost gone. "You don't want her if she's just after the money, son. But, on the other hand, you don't deserve her if you can't tell her the truth. Both of you have a heap of thinking to do. I'm going to do you a big favor, Jason. I'm changing my will. You'll get the money, but not for ten years."

"You're right, Grandpa. I need to make my own way in life. You did."

Mixed male tears fall on white hospital linens. Painfully, Karl sits upright and embraces his grandson with all the strength he has left. A young nurse waits patiently with Karl's medication.

Jason leaves the hospital, calls Miranda out of the salon and tells her the truth. "You don't know the real Jason Weber, but I promise I'll show him to you if you want to stick around."

Her eyes punish him. "You're a fraud, Jason. Don't call me!" She pushes him away.

It's over.

212

The black SUV goes up for sale. Jason works hard to get out of debt.

Several months later, a card arrives.

Dear Jason:

It's hard for me to write you. I'm a bit shy. You don't know me, although we talked a few times at the hospital. I'm one of the nurses that cared for your grandpa Karl. I miss him terribly. Would you call me sometime? I'd like to get to know another genuine Weber.

Amanda Carlson

P.S. I love hiking. Your grandpa told me about your secret trout fishing spot on Deer Creek.

Standing
on his snakeskin boots

"More presents? What are you trying to do, make me feel guilty?"

"No, Lexie. I've just got this need to be a grandfather. It's all I can think about. Are you guys still trying?"

Nick Dailey is standing on the wide front porch of his daughter's new house with two packages in his arms, one wrapped in shiny blue foil and the other in pink tissue.

Lexie sits down on a white patio chair, accepts the gifts and hesitantly pulls back the wrappings.

"When you want something, you're so predictable, Dad. Miniature wooden trains and fluffy, white teddy bears won't get you a grandchild."

"Maybe it's my age. I know I've been a terrible father. I want to have a second chance to do it right."

Lexie, now thirty-eight and married, is Nick's only child. She's from his first marriage. He's had two wives since.

"I did send you presents," he offers.

"I remember," she says. "Parcels in the mail with white teddy bears and notes reading 'Daddy loves you.'" She pauses. "But most of my life I've been fatherless. I never had a daddy to read to me at night or fix the basket on my bike or walk me to school."

He hangs his head. "I did visit."

"Sure. From time to time, you'd resurface and tell me you were sorry, and I wanted to believe you. You'd stand there on the front porch, shifting from one foot to another, while Mom glared at you. I remember standing on your old snakeskin boots so I could reach up and hug you. I loved the feel of your rough face and hands." She turns away. "And then you'd be gone, and I wouldn't see you for months."

Nick is now living alone in the yellow trailer he's always lived in. He still spray-paints cars for people in the metal shop out back. The familiar odor of paint thinner lingers in his hair.

Lexie stands rigid and faces him with her arms folded. "If you disappear again, Dad, it's over. I'm not some unfeeling object you can just pick up whenever you feel fatherly stirrings. You're lucky I even talk to you."

"I'll be the most amazing grandfather you could ever imagine, sweetheart. I'll babysit any time you ask. I'll never forget a birthday. I'll teach your kids how to ride a two-wheeler, and I'll build a tire swing in your backyard."

Nick stops and looks at his daughter. Lexie is a confident career woman with an upper-level position in a national media company. She can melt metal with her green eyes when she's angry. Her shiny, auburn hair has a fuss-free business cut, and she's wearing a designer suit and Gucci shoes. It's hard to picture her in fuzzy slippers and a chenille robe nursing a baby in front of the fireplace.

"Lexie, I need another chance. I'll never let you down if you give me a grandchild. Please."

She slowly picks up the presents. "You might as well take these back."

Nick staggers in disbelief. "Are you punishing me for being a bad father?"

Lexie puts both her hands on her father's trembling shoulders. "I can't make you a grandfather, Dad. We just got the news. My doctor says it's impossible."

He chokes. "I'll never get another chance to be a real father?"

Then, with tears welling up, she slips off her shoes. She pulls her father close and steps on his snakeskin boots like she did as a little girl.

"You can be a real father again, Dad."

"How? Are you adopting?"

"No, Dad. You can be a real father to me...I've been waiting all my life."

That wing's got to go

Del Owens is dozing on the green leather sofa after his birthday dinner. His mouth is open, and his head is tilted to one side. Long strands of gray hair are hanging over the edge of the sofa.

"Does Dad even know how stupid that thing looks?" asks his oldest son from the kitchen.

"He's a bald man in denial," comments his other son. "I've watched him adjusting his masterpiece, pulling that clump of hair over from the side and gluing it to his scalp with hair grease. The way he was patting it and tilting his head in front of the mirror, you could tell he thought it looked good."

His daughter Roxanne whispers around the corner, "We should bribe his barber to make a mistake with the clippers next time. That side wing has got to go."

Brendan, Del's five-year-old grandson, is kneeling beside the coffee table cutting up foil wrapping paper.

Without warning, he slides over next to his grandfather's head and snips off the dangling strands. He stands up and carries the trophy into the kitchen. "Look, Mommy. I cut off Grandpa's hair wing."

Everybody gasps, and nobody wants to touch it. Where do you put the severed evidence of Grandpa's denial? Do you hide it in the garbage? Stretch it out on a paper towel? Will he want it back?

The commotion in the kitchen wakes Del.

He stretches, then sits up. Unconsciously, his right hand reaches to adjust the strands he has grown to cover his baldness. His fingers feel only a stiff tuft.

Del runs to the bathroom with his hands covering his scalp. Angrily, he yells through the locked door, "Roxanne, you've gone too far! You may think it's funny, but I've never said a word when you've gone from being a redhead to a blonde to a brunette, all in the same year."

"Dad, calm down. Why are you accusing me? Brendan did it. That wing hanging down beside a little kid with a pair of scissors was just too much temptation."

Everyone gathers outside the bathroom door.

Del's voice rises. "I've had this classic hairstyle since I was sixteen, tapered on the sides and parted on the left. It will take me a year to grow it back. I've got a meeting first thing in the morning at the bank. I'll look like an idiot going in there like this."

His oldest son steps outside and calls their family barber at home. "Little Andy" has cut Del's hair for thirty years.

"Sorry to bother you so late, Andy, but we've got a family emergency here. Can you open the shop for us?"

Andy replies sarcastically, "What happened? Somebody's hair grow over their nose and mouth so they can't breathe? If you've got an emergency, call 911. I ain't opening up at 9:30 at night for nobody."

"Listen, Andy. My dad's paid you hundreds of times. We really need your help."

Little Andy finally agrees.

Back in the house, Del's grandson pleads through the bathroom door, "I'm sorry, Grandpa. I hope your skinny hair will grow long again."

All the males in Del's family arrive at Little Andy's barbershop at 10:00 p.m. Andy takes one look and clicks the guard onto his clippers. "This'll take a buzz cut."

As Del enters the bank the next morning, a young teller motions him over. "New hairstyle, Mr. Owens?" She winks. "It makes you look a lot younger!"

He smiles and pulls out a photo of himself, his sons and his grandson in the barber shop. "All the guys got buzz cuts yesterday. It was for a good cause."

Note behind the chair

Julie jams a crowbar behind the old "Outgoing Mail" cabinet in the office of the head mistress.

As the varnished mahogany breaks away, a discolored manila envelope stuck behind it falls to the floor.

Rod and Julie Davis own SP Architectural Salvage. They are dismantling the old Hillside Girls School on 41st Avenue.

As Julie scoops up the envelope, she notices a memo written in perfect penmanship: "Confiscated for her own good." Inside are several smaller, light blue envelopes. She stuffs them all into her overalls and continues removing the old cabinetry.

After dinner, she lays the envelopes on the kitchen table—three letters, all addressed to "William Edwards." The return address is "Victoria Hayden, Hillside Girls Residential School." All are stamped, but there are no postmarks. Small red hearts are drawn on the backs of the envelopes.

"I need to find William Edwards," Julie says.

Rod shakes his head. "You'll mess up someone's life. Those letters were hidden for a reason. Leave it alone."

"But we've located people before when we found valuables in old buildings. I think these letters are valuable."

Within a week, using the Internet and property records, Julie locates William.

She calls and tells him about the letters. Widowed for three years, he agrees to meet her in a coffee shop.

William accepts the letters awkwardly. Not knowing what to say, he opens one and reads:

I wasn't sure if you would answer my first letter. Did you get it? Please don't hate me for writing you.

At yesterday's practice for the inter-school Christmas musical, I stood behind you, in the first row of the choir. You turned around and smiled, but then you just put your trombone in its case and left.

I know you might not be interested in me because of my leg, but polio doesn't mean I'm not normal in every other way.

If you want to meet me sometime, leave a note for me behind your chair at next week's practice.

William is silent. Julie waits for his response.

"I do remember her. Very pretty girl, long brown hair, leg brace. Polio."

"Did you ever ask her out?"

"No. We went to different schools. I only saw her at inter-school music practices. She smiled at me but never said anything. I didn't know if she was shy or stuck up. Couldn't figure her out."

"You never received any letters from her?"

William shakes his head. "Never."

"Why would someone confiscate the letters?"

William shrugs. "In those days, school officials were much more concerned with protecting students in their care. People who had physical disabilities were often made fun of. Maybe the school was trying to protect Victoria from being hurt."

"Would you have asked her out if you had known about the letters?"

William has a faraway look in his eye.

He nods. "Probably no way of finding her now."

Julie smiles. "Apparently, she still has the same last name. The administrator I talked to at the new Hillside School told me Victoria was a librarian at a university for forty years and retired last summer."

One week later, as Victoria Hayden sorts through her mail, she finds a letter from "William Edwards." Old feelings of hurt and rejection surface, but she must open it, and does.

Dear Victoria:

I just received your letters after all these years. We have much to talk about.

Would you join me on the evening of the 31st at the Commonwealth Theatre? The Hillside School choir and concert band have their dress rehearsal performance that evening.

William Edwards

P.S. Please consider this my belated "note behind the chair."

She needs the money for a brake job

Last week, Joanne got some disturbing news. She's getting used to disturbing news.

"Your van's brakes are unsafe, Mrs. Ross. I can't allow you to drive it any further." The serviceman hands her an estimate. It's three hundred dollars she doesn't have.

Joanne is forty, raising two young teenagers. Her uncooperative ex-husband left recently. She's been a stay-at-home mom, looking after everybody. Now that her husband is with his new woman, she's left with almost nothing.

Three mornings a week, she goes downtown to fill out job applications at the employment center, hoping for a chance to get back on her feet.

Should she try to borrow the money from her brother?

He's always so condescending: "Joanne, we all make choices in life. I warned you about Blaine when you married him."

It's spring, and yard sale signs are popping up. A garage sale might raise enough money for the brake job.

At 8:00 a.m. on Saturday morning, her signs are up, but it's raining.

Seasoned "early birds" have come and gone, disgusted that she'd even bother to put up a sign for what little she had to sell.

By one o'clock, Joanne has taken in only $103. She's discouraged and finally brings out some family memories that she really didn't want to part with: a box of her dad's fishing gear and a suitcase filled with Fisher-Price toys.

A few minutes later, a middle-aged man pulls up in a brown Dodge truck with a boat on top.

"Hi. Anything good here?"

He seems a friendly sort.

"Are you a fisherman?" Joanne drags forward the dusty box from the back of the garage. "My father bought fishing stuff when he could afford it. Mom let him. Fishing made him happy."

The sight of her dad's old fly rods brings back memories. "Daddy used to get me up at sunrise to go down to the trout pond. I was his 'detangler,' getting the hooks out of the trees when his casts were crooked. Sometimes he'd yell, 'Help me with this monster! I can't handle him by myself!' Then together we'd bring in a feisty, little rainbow trout."

She blushes, embarrassed at having told all this to a stranger.

The man smiles. "I love old fly rods. I'll give you two hundred bucks for everything in the box."

She's stunned. Twenty dollars would have been fair. Now she's got the money for her brake job. Thank God for fishermen.

He gives her a check signed "Bernie Weaver." She hesitates before accepting and makes a note of his license plate number.

An hour later, as Joanne is taking down her sign, Bernie Weaver drives up and unloads the box of fly fishing equipment. "I need to return this to you. Could I please have my check back?"

Joanne bursts into tears. "You have to keep those fishing rods! I need the money!"

Bernie hands her a slip of paper. "Call this man. I stopped in to see him after I left here. He knows about this stuff. You sold me an H.L. Leonard split bamboo fly rod. It went for a hundred dollars back in 1955, and it's worth ten times that today. The other stuff's the same. He's prepared to buy everything in this box for collectors' prices."

Joanne is shocked. "But why did you bring everything back?"

Bernie looks serious. "You trusted me enough to take my check. And when you told me that story about your father, I felt like I knew him. I just couldn't cheat the daughter of another fly fisherman."

Christmas for a garbage man's wife

"You're not coming here for Christmas, Sammy. You threw away your rights the last time you got busted."

"I'm tryin' so hard, Tara. I'm sendin' you all the extra cash I got. I'm not hangin' around with Gino no more. You and Connor are all that matter to me now."

She closes her apartment door and snaps the deadbolts into place. Then, through the locked door: "Your son needs a real father."

Sammy Diaz has been out of prison for six months.

Can he change? Deserted at eight by a violent, alcoholic father. Always moving with a loving, narcotic-addicted mother who never paid her rent on time. His childhood memories are of Christmas mornings in women's shelters.

He wants a real Christmas this year, with a tree and gifts for his wife and son, bought with his own money earned from his new job as a garbage man. He's just not making enough yet.

The city manager hires ex-cons who want a second chance. "People can change. Those who want to can get an opportunity from me."

On Tuesday, his past greets him from a parked car on Conway Street. "Hey, Sammy. Need a few extra bucks?"

It's Gino.

"We're doin' phony cards again. Need a bunch of new IDs by Friday. You got the trash, we got the cash. You in?"

"Identity thieves" mine residential garbage for credit card and social security numbers. Within twenty-four hours, your identification can be for sale with someone else's photograph.

An ex-con driving a garbage truck makes a natural partner. He knows the trash profile of everyone on his route. Some don't use shredders—easy pickings. Nobody suspects the garbage man.

Sammy's tempted. A thousand dollars cash by Christmas would be perfect. After his rent, his bills and the money he sends Tara every month, there's nothing left.

With a razor knife, he slices a few bags, just for curiosity. One in five has usable numbers.

It would be so easy. But he just can't forget his three-year-old son waving from the balcony the last time he drove away.

Friday comes. Gino calls for the numbers. Sammy hesitates. "Maybe next time."

But temptation comes in many forms.

There's a frail, old lady on his route who always puts her garbage in two white plastic bags. Vegetable peels, eggshells, tea bags and leftovers in one bag. Newspapers, bottles and cans in the other. Sammy knows she's too old to understand recycling, so he always takes the second bag in the truck with him to put into the recycling bin back at the yard.

A week before Christmas, she puts out three bags. Sammy takes two into the cab, thinking they're both for recycling.

The third bag feels unusual. He opens it and finds a man's history in brown bags and tattered envelopes.

Medals, diaries, photographs and $740 in cash. This lady's husband had been a fighter pilot during the war.

$740 would be enough to give Tara and Connor the Christmas he's hoped for.

*****

Christmas Eve in Tara's tiny apartment. Blinking colored lights. A decorated tree sheltering gifts in shiny paper.

She smiles at her young son. "It's OK, Connor. Open your present from Daddy. He worked extra hard this year so he could buy us things."

Tara throws her arms around her husband. "I love the necklace, Sammy."

On the refrigerator door, a newspaper clipping: "Cash from Trash: Honest garbage man rescues priceless memories and cash. Receives generous reward from family and big raise from boss."

Clunk

"Welcome to Wrangler's. May I take your order?"

"I'll have a Texas burger with extra sauce and a large black coffee."

Lucas Miller pulls ahead to the pick-up window. He hands the cashier a ten-dollar bill. As he pays, the teenaged girl hesitates, not wanting to touch his mutilated hand.

It's always the same. Everyone's repelled by the scarred and mangled flesh that used to be his left hand.

It happened ten years ago, the summer he turned sixteen, on his first shift at the sawmill.

A rough 2X10 had jammed on the slow-moving, green chain. Inexperienced and not thinking, he reached over to free it. His left hand was caught by the unguarded chain and sprocket, and his whole arm was pulled into the screeching conveyor.

The last words he heard before passing out on the sawdust were: "Shut the chain down. The Miller kid's lost his hand!"

The surgeons did the best they could. His thumb and three fingers are gone. They saved part of his palm and most of his baby finger.

Now he's a freak of sorts.

Children stare. "Look at his ugly hand, Mommy. Why is it broken like that?"

He has trouble dating. In some ways, it would be better if he had lost the hand completely.

Winter is his favorite time, the colder the better. Everyone's wearing gloves or mitts. That's when he feels normal again.

Lucas loves to ski. It's good he didn't lose a leg.

One Saturday afternoon at the mountain, he's separated from his friends and ends up as a "single" in the line-up for the chairlift. He joins three other skiers on the chair: an elderly couple and an attractive girl in her mid-twenties.

He introduces himself. "I'm Lucas Miller. Do you folks ski here often?"

"Every winter," the elderly gentleman replies. "We're here on vacation from the prairies."

The ride to the top takes ten minutes. They all enjoy pleasant conversation.

As they unload, the grandmother suggests, "Amy, maybe you would like to ski with this nice young man. We're slowing you down, I'm sure."

Lucas and Amy ski their first run together. She keeps up with him.

"You're pretty good for a girl from the flat lands," he remarks.

She pushes off ahead of him. "My family's been coming here since I was nine. We look forward to this all year."

As they ride up the chair together for the last run of the day, Amy touches his arm. "It's not like Granny to leave me with a strange man on the mountain. She must have a good feeling about you."

He replies, "I don't go out with girls much. Maybe your grandmother could tell."

Amy is puzzled. "Why?"

He avoids the question. "Can I buy you a hot chocolate?"

"Yes, I'd like that. My foot is really cold."

Inside the lodge, she takes off her goggles and ski hat, revealing her long, auburn hair and deep brown eyes. Lucas is spellbound.

Amy lifts one leg onto the bench beside her. "Can you please help me with this ski boot?"

That's when she notices his hand. "What happened?"

He tells her the story.

Then, Lucas unbuckles her ski boot. As her foot slides out, it hits the floor with a clunk.

Lucas slowly looks up at her. Their eyes meet. "What happencd, Amy?"

"I lost my leg two years ago in a farm machinery accident."

As they walk to the cateteria together, Amy takes his hand.

With her hiking boots on, she has a noticeable limp.

A crooked eye

The smelly, greasy-haired man pulls open the heavy glass door of the bus depot as travelers come and go. The crooked eye above his crushed cheekbone is unable to blink.

"Merry Christmas, ma'am, and you, too, young lady. Could ya spare some change for a hot drink?"

The well-dressed older woman standing uncertainly inside the door and clutching the hand of a young girl bursts into tears.

"Don't cry here." The man looks fearfully towards the ticket counter. "I didn't do nothin' to ya."

The woman sniffs back her tears. "Someone stole my purse with our bus tickets. I don't know how my granddaughter and I are going to get home. I don't know a soul in this city, and I can't reach my daughter by phone. The bus company won't help me, and I don't know what to do. We'll be out on the street tonight. We won't survive. We're not used to it."

The homeless man in the buttonless beige trench coat touches a bandaged hand to his soiled leather hat and says quietly, "I'm sorry to have bothered ya. The way you're dressed I thought you might be able to help a fella."

Then, his face softens into a gap-toothed smile. "I'm awful sorry about the tickets. I hope ya find your way back home. I'd help ya, but got myself down to nothin' right now."

It's December 23. Barbara Mercer has taken the bus three hundred miles to pick up her granddaughter Gabriella for Christmas. Gabriella was sent to this city on another bus by her divorced mother, who was leaving to spend Christmas with her new boyfriend.

The depot will close in an hour when the last bus leaves.

The icy wind has picked up, and the front door flies open repeatedly. The homeless man steadies the banging door for customers as they enter. He holds out a faded paper coffee cup and asks hopefully, "Help someone out tonight?"

Finally, the ticket agent comes out from behind the counter, takes several steps toward the door and yells at the homeless man. "Darrel, you dirt bag, nobody wants your help with the door. Leave."

Barbara paces in front of the ticket counter, questioning the agent between customers. "You wouldn't force us to sleep on the street tonight? That's really your company's policy on stolen tickets?"

The agent throws up his hands. "Lady, I've got no way of knowing you even had a ticket. If I gave tickets to everyone who said they lost theirs, the buses would be full of bums like Darrel there. I told you to call the cops."

Barbara hangs her head. "I did, but they said they were too busy tonight to send someone out."

Forty-five minutes pass. Barbara stares fearfully at her sleeping granddaughter.

Suddenly, "Darrel the doorman" rushes in, heading straight for Barbara and her granddaughter.

Gabriella wakes with a start and shrinks back from the stench.

"Merry Christmas, ladies," says Darrel and hands his folded-over paper cup to Barbara. "Old lady in a fur coat just rolled down her window and handed me a wad. Told me to get some shelter tonight, but I know it's meant for you. Your tickets home." His crooked eye fills with water.

When the ticket agent arrives in the morning to open up on the busiest day of the year, he's faced with a major inconvenience. A lifeless form curled up in a filthy, red sleeping bag lies in the icy doorway.

The coroner is called and records the death as "exposure."

As they pick up the body, the top of the sleeping bag falls away. The warm morning sun touches a crooked eye.

CPSIA information can be obtained
at www.ICGtesting.com
Printed in the USA
LVHW020521260523
748105LV00004B/8